Praise for Michael A. Kahn

THE DEAD HAND
The Tenth Rachel Gold Mystery

"A high-water mark in this inventive, ebullient series."
—*Kirkus Reviews*

"Kahn, a lawyer with a good sense of humor, uses a light touch to make complicated points of law accessible and even enjoyable as mystery fare."
—*Booklist*

"A practicing trial attorney, Michael A. Kahn is one of the few authors who continues to make courtroom scenes absolutely delightful."
—*Kings River Life* magazine

FACE VALUE
The Ninth Rachel Gold Mystery

"Ample humor and skillful dialogue—about legal, financial, and scientific matters—are a plus, as is the expertly evoked St. Louis locale."
—*Publishers Weekly*

"Rachel's fans will enjoy her latest case, which highlights the consequences of greed as well as the abilities of the disabled."
—*Booklist*

THE FLINCH FACTOR
The Eighth Rachel Gold Mystery

"A clever, engrossing legal thriller."
—Scott Turow, #1 *New York Times* bestselling author

"Legal mystery aficionados will be pleased to see St. Louis attorney Rachel Gold back again after a long absence."
—*Library Journal*

"Readers will enjoy the skillful blend of suspense and humor."
—*Booklist*

"A trial lawyer himself, Kahn handles the legal details briskly."
—*Publishers Weekly*

TROPHY WIDOW
The Seventh Rachel Gold Mystery

"Totally enthralling and believable. The plot is so complex and multi-layered that the audience won't have a clue whom the guilty party is until the author chooses to reveal it. *Trophy Widow* is a must read for anyone who likes a top-rate thriller."
—*Midwest Book*

"Gold can't resist getting drawn in, and readers may feel the same way about this latest legal thriller in Michael A. Kahn's Rachel Gold series, which shows off his trademark lightning repartee and captivating setup."
—*Publishers Weekly*

"It's a treat to see Rachel back from her extended leave of absence since *Sheer Gall* (1996), and working such a meaty, satisfying case as this one."

—*Kirkus Reviews*

BEARING WITNESS
The Sixth Rachel Gold Mystery

"*Bearing Witness* grips you from the start. If you have not read Michael Kahn's terrific legal thrillers before, you are in for a treat."
—Philip Margolin, *New York Times* bestselling author

"The cagey attorney with 'the mind of Brandeis and the stems of a showgirl' is once again the alluring, and very human, heart of Mike Kahn's latest stellar effort. I stipulate that even the lawyer-bashing Republicans in Congress will doff their caps in praise."
—James Warren, *Chicago Tribune*

"Michael Kahn's Rachel Gold is among the most interesting of contemporary fictional characters. In *Bearing Witness*, she explores a dark and seldom-mentioned past."
—John Lutz, *New York Times* bestselling author

"In this compelling thriller, Kahn makes good use of historical material and offers a revealing look at Orthodox Judaism. Rachel Gold and her eclectic entourage deserve more attention."
—*Booklist*

"Kahn's likable characters and well-managed plots make this entertaining read a solid addition to its series."
—*Publishers Weekly*

SHEER GALL
The Fifth Rachel Gold Mystery

"A sheer delight! Fast and funny. I couldn't get enough. Fans of Rachel Gold rejoice!"

—Tamar Myers, bestselling author

"The combination of lawyerly wisdom, first-rate writing, and a compelling plot."

—*Legal Times*

"*Sheer Gall* has it all. Rachel Gold is one of the great characters in contemporary fiction."

—*Tulsa World*

"Gold digs deep into the surprising market for animal byproducts in an intricate, suspenseful story."

—*Publishers Weekly*

DUE DILIGENCE
The Fourth Rachel Gold Mystery

"Quite definitely addictive…a must-read, written with wit and humor and peopled with multidimensional characters. What more could a reader ask for? I love Rachel Gold—her independence and tough-mindedness, intelligence, and wit."

—Mary Balogh, *New York Times* bestselling author

"A clever, high-spirited thriller…Rachel's first-person narration is intelligent and breezy, and she's supported by a memorable secondary cast."

—*Publishers Weekly*

"An intricate plot, witty dialogue, and memorable characters... fine reading."

—*Booklist*

FIRM AMBITIONS
The Third Rachel Gold Mystery

"Rachel remains one of the more engaging sleuths on the mystery scene."

—*Publishers Weekly*

"Good narrative and a great read."

—*Library Journal*

"Her latest case—starting with sex, drugs, and gambling, and then getting really dirty—is a beaut."

—*Kirkus Reviews*

"Clever, wonderful, delicious...don't miss it."

—*St. Louis Post-Dispatch*

DEATH BENEFITS
The Second Rachel Gold Mystery

"A fresh-voiced heroine, down-and-dirty legal detail, and more honest detection than you'd expect make this a winner."

—*Kirkus Reviews*

"Superb... Vividly portrayed... A real page-turner."

—*San Diego Jewish Times*

"Chicanery, avarice, sexual happenings, and big-city life... fast-moving."

—*Mystery Times*

GRAVE DESIGNS
The First Rachel Gold Mystery

"With an ear for intelligent, breezy dialogue and clever plotting, Kahn spins an engrossing yarn."
—Publishers Weekly

"A Ludlum-esque thriller…an imaginative, fast-paced winner… twists to keep you hanging on to your seat."
—San Antonio Express-News

"An absorbing page-turner."
—Jewish Light

"An engrossing plot, credible characters, and an abundance of sparkling wit…a delight."
—Anchorage Times

PLAYED!

"Fans of quick reads like James Patterson's popular BookShots series will be well served by this thriller's fast pace."
—Library Journal

"The outcome is never in much doubt in this pleasant tale built on the love between two brothers."
—Publishers Weekly

"Ornaments of the Missouri bar attacking, undermining, and double-crossing each other provides brisk, sprightly entertainment, and the hapless defendant's baseball background comes into play just when it's most needed."
—Kirkus Reviews

THE SIRENA QUEST

"Equal parts rollicking adventure, existential and spiritual quest, and coming-of-(middle)-age tale, this stand-alone set in 1994 from Kahn includes a cameo appearance from series lead Rachel Gold."

—*Publishers Weekly*

"Michael A. Kahn provides an exciting treasure hunt thriller enhanced by deep metaphysical middle-age identity crises."

—*Midwest Book Review*

Also by Michael A. Kahn

Rachel Gold Mysteries
The Dead Hand
Face Value
Flinch Factor
Trophy Widow
Bearing Witness
Sheer Gall
Due Diligence
Firm Ambitions
Death Benefits
Grave Designs

Other Novels
Played!
The Sirena Quest
The Mourning Sexton (under the name Michael Baron)
The Art of Conflict (with Alan Kohn)

BAD TRUST

BAD TRUST

AN ATTORNEY RACHEL GOLD MYSTERY

MICHAEL A. KAHN

Poisoned Pen
PRESS

Published by Poisoned Pen Press, an imprint of Sourcebooks
P.O. Box 4410, Naperville, Illinois 60567-4410
(630) 961-3900
sourcebooks.com

Library of Congress Cataloging-in-Publication data is on file with the publisher.

Printed and bound in the United States of America.
SB 10 9 8 7 6 5 4 3 2 1

To Margi—again and always

"They were conquerors, and for that you want only brute force—nothing to boast of, when you have it, since your strength is just an accident arising from the weakness of others."
—Joseph Conrad, *Heart of Darkness*

"If you want to know what God thinks of money, just look at the people he gave it to."
—Dorothy Parker

Chapter One

"I have a better idea. Let's have him killed."

"Oh, my God, Megan. Don't say such things."

Megan turned toward her sister, eyebrows raised, and shook her head. "Come on, Holly. Who are you kidding? You know we'd both be better off with him dead."

Holly gave me an embarrassed shrug. "That's my big sister talking. Not me."

"Right." Megan grinned. "That's your big sister talking— saying the same damn words you'd be saying if you weren't little Miss Prim-and-Proper."

"That's not true, Megan."

I raised my hands, palms facing them. "Time out, ladies. I'm your lawyer, not your hit man."

Megan laughed. "Sorry, Rachel. My bad. It's just sometimes I get so upset over what that bastard is doing to us—and to our children—that I'd like to kill him."

"I understand your anger." I nodded toward the trust documents spread out on my desk. "There's plenty of money here. More than enough for the two of you and for your children."

"Absolutely. You have the last brokerage statement there. Shows more than twelve million dollars in that trust fund—money our father put in there for each of us. And that rich self-centered prick won't give us a goddamn dime."

"She's right, Rachel," Holly said. "We've both asked our brother. More than once."

This was the initial client meeting. Think of it as the legal profession's equivalent of a blind date, with each side trying to assess the prospects of entering a genuine relationship. Do I want to represent these people, the lawyer asks? Do I trust them? Do I want to go to war on their behalf? And the potential client asks, Do I want this lawyer to represent me? Do I trust her? Does she seem tough enough to be my advocate?

What makes someone seek out a lawyer? In my experience, it's either anger or distress, and here I had one of each. Megan Garber and Holly Goodman were sisters in their early forties, both mothers of two teenage daughters. And studies in contrasts.

Megan, forty-three, was a big woman, perhaps twenty pounds north of voluptuous, which in her high heels gave her stride a tottering quality. She had straight black hair cut shoulder-length and parted on the side, which accented her high cheekbones, prominent nose, and sharp chin.

Holly, forty-one, was slimmer and prettier than her older sister, although I'd hesitate to wager money on the original color of her wavy blond hair or the original shape of her cute pug nose, especially when compared to the same two features on her older sister and brother. Holly had a gentler, more vulnerable persona than her sister, best exemplified by their laughs. Megan was a horse laugher, head thrown back, hand slapping her knee. Holly was a giggler, with a hand over her mouth.

Although their stylish outfits, makeup, and jewelry pegged them as a pair of luncheon habitués at The Zodiac at Neiman-Marcus, neither woman was wealthy, both had jobs, and both were no longer married—Megan by choice, Holly by fate.

Megan Garber's marriage ended in the nasty aftermath of her husband Larry's affair with his secretary. At the time of the divorce, Larry Garber was a partner in a midsize local law firm. Two years later, a national law firm acquired his firm, and two years after that the national firm laid off six lawyers in the St. Louis office, including Larry, who's now a struggling solo practitioner. His income had fallen to such an extent that he was able to convince the family court judge to reduce his alimony and child support payments, forcing Megan to seek employment after more than a decade out of the workforce. She is now a sales associate at the Pottery Barn in Plaza Frontenac.

Holly Goodman became a widow five years ago. Her husband, Marc, like most men and women in their midthirties, assumed he had a long life ahead of him, and thus made no transition plans for Goodman Jewelry, the business he'd inherited from his father. Nor had he worried about the significant debt his company took on for the construction of a new store on Clayton Road in upscale Ladue, instead assuming he'd pay it down over the years. But two weeks after his thirty-sixth birthday, he was diagnosed with bone sarcoma. Five months later he was dead. Within a year of his death, Goodman Jewelry had imploded, with most of its inventory auctioned off in a liquidation sale. Holly, who'd earned a master's in social work at the University of Missouri, now worked as a school social worker in the Lindbergh school district.

"He's a nasty bastard, Rachel," Megan said. "Here's the latest example. My daughter Lauren starts college in the fall. At Northwestern. Do you have *any* idea how much a year of college costs these days?"

"Actually, I do. I have a stepdaughter at Johns Hopkins. So you asked your brother for a distribution from the trust?"

"Yep."

"And?"

Megan shook her head. "First off, I never get to talk to him. My own brother—my only goddamn brother—and yet I have to talk to either his witch or his weasel. This time it was the weasel."

"The Weasel." I smiled. "That would be Arnold Bell?"

"Yep. So I gave that conniving little brown-nose a copy of the bill for tuition, room, and board. For the first semester. More than thirty grand. I told him to remind his boss that my daughter also happens to be his niece."

"And?"

"Unbelievable." She opened her purse, sorted through the contents, and held up a folded sheet of paper. "This arrived two days later."

She slid it across the desk to me. It was a printout of an email from Arnold Bell to Megan Garber. The subject line read:

Re: Request for Disbursement from Peggy R. Blumenthal Trust.

The text consisted of two sentences:

After conscientious and solemn consideration and contem-plation by the Trustee, your above-referenced disbursement request has been deemed premature and is thus declined. In the interim, the Trustee instructs me to wish you *sholom aleichem*.

I looked up, struggling to hide my emotions. I try my best in these initial client meetings to be neutral—to gather the facts, to explore the issues, to gauge the prospective clients, and, at the conclusion, to explain that I will take it all under advisement and get back to them in a few days. But whatever lingering misgivings I might have had about leading this battle vanished upon reading that passive-aggressive email from their brother's lackey.

Holly pointed toward the email printout. "Can I see?"

I handed it to her. She read the message. "That's just not right."

She looked down again at the message and looked up at me with a frown. "What does that mean at the end, Rachel? Those two words."

"It's a Yiddish blessing. It means 'peace be with you.'"

"Peace be with us?" Megan snorted. "More like piece of shit be with us. Like I said, we'd both be better off with him dead."

Chapter Two

"Oy." Benny shook his head. "What was that douchebag's name before he changed it?"

"Alan Blumenthal."

"And now?"

"You ready? Isaiah ben Moishe."

"Moishe? Who the fuck is Moishe?"

"I'm only guessing, Benny. His dad's name was Milton. Maybe Moishe was his Hebrew name."

"And Isaiah?"

I shrugged. "No idea. Maybe the prophet?"

"Really? I'd say that's a bit delusional."

"Or maybe the basketball player?"

"Isaiah Thomas? That's even more delusional."

"True."

"So, is this guy a real frummie?"

"You mean an Orthodox Jew? I suppose, but I did a little calling around, trying to find out which synagogue he belongs to."

"And?"

"I came up empty."

Benny rubbed his chin as he thought it over. "Maybe he just likes that Prophet Isaiah vibe."

"What do you mean?"

"Your guy sounds like a real prick. Think back to all those Yom Kippur services. Specifically, the reading of the Haftorah. Isaiah is the Darth Vader of the High Holidays, right? He is one dark, brooding motherfucker, issuing condemnations of the people and predictions of doom."

Benny leaned back in his chair and squinted at the ceiling. "I can still recall one of those screeds about all the sinners. How they lie and cheat and give birth to evil. Something about hatching the eggs of vipers. Right?"

"Vaguely."

Benny chuckled. "Isaiah ain't exactly the Mister Rogers of the Yom Kippur."

A pair of young servers arrived—a woman and a man, both of Asian descent. We were having lunch at Pho Grand, our favorite Vietnamese restaurant—a stylish bistro with Asian string instruments mounted in glass along pastel yellow walls.

"*Pho Tai?*" the young woman asked.

I raised my hand. "That's me."

I watched, my mouth watering, as she set down a large steaming bowl of rice noodle soup with sliced beef. Next to the bowl she placed a platter heaped with bean sprouts, Thai basil leaves, cilantro, lime wedges, and chili peppers.

The male server had set his large tray of entrees on a stand and was now frowning as he looked at our table and then at the tray and then back at our table. "The *Bun Bi Cha Gio?*"

Benny gave a him a thumbs-up. "Me."

The server set down the large plate of vermicelli noodles with eggrolls, shredded pork skin, and vegetables.

He straightened, looked back at his tray, and turned to us. "The *Banh Cuon Thit Nuong?*"

"Me, again, dude."

And the server set down, next to Benny's other entrée, a platter of rice flour crepes filled with ground pork, mushrooms, and onions, and topped with charbroiled pork and fried onions.

"And that beef stir-fry," Benny said to him. "Mine, too."

With raised eyebrows, the server set down the third entrée in front of Benny. Then he backed up, smiled, and said, "Enjoy."

Among his many unique qualities, Benny Goldberg has capacity.

And girth.

And brains to match.

We met more than a decade ago as first-year associates in the Chicago offices of Abbott & Windsor. A few years later, we both escaped that LaSalle Street sweatshop—Benny to teach law at DePaul, me to go solo as Rachel Gold, Attorney at Law. Different reasons brought us to St. Louis. For me, it was a yearning to live closer to my mother after my father died. For Benny, a year later, it was an offer he couldn't refuse from the Washington University School of Law.

Although in the years since then, Professor Benjamin Goldberg has earned a national reputation in the field of trade-regulation law—you may have seen him quoted in the *Wall Street Journal* or interviewed on CNBC—he remains my beloved Benny: vulgar, fat, gluttonous, and rowdy. But also ferociously loyal and wonderfully funny and my very best friend in the whole world. I love him like the brother I never had.

"No class today?" I asked.

"Actually, have one this afternoon. My advanced antitrust seminar."

"Really? And you're going to class dressed like that?"

"*Moi?*" He leaned back in his chair and gestured at his outfit. "What's wrong with this, Miss Fashion Cop?"

Benny had on a New York Rangers hockey jersey, faded olive cargo pants, and red Converse Chuck Taylor All Star low tops. His shaggy Jew-fro had reached Jimi Hendrix proportions, and he apparently hadn't shaved that morning. Not quite the prevailing image for an esteemed legal scholar.

I shook my head. "All I can say is thank God for tenure."

"Hear, hear." He grinned and raised his bottle of Tsingtao.

When Benny had finished his first plate and signaled the waiter for another beer, he turned to me with a puzzled smile. "Isaiah, eh? When did that happen?"

"A few years ago. I'm not sure of the exact date."

"So it was after he destroyed his old man?"

"That's my understanding. A couple years later."

Isaiah (né Alan) is the eldest of three siblings—Megan and Holly being the other two—and thus the only son of Milton and Peggy Blumenthal. A few years before Alan's birth their father had founded a little scrap-iron company under the name MP Enterprises—the M for Milton and the P for Peggy. The business had grown exponentially over the years. By the time Alan joined the company, after earning his law degree from Washington University, MP Enterprises owned a diverse portfolio of companies in various industries around the country.

"When did the company go public?" Benny asked.

"About ten years ago, on the thirtieth anniversary of its founding."

At the time, Milton was CEO and chairman of the board, and Alan was vice president and general counsel. The public offering made both men multimillionaires.

In the story that ran in the St. Louis Post-Dispatch the day after MP Enterprises went public, Milton told the reporter, "I consider myself the luckiest man on the face of this earth." He may not have realized that he was quoting baseball great Lou Gehrig, who died less than two years after delivering that poignant farewell speech in Yankee Stadium on July 4, 1939. Nor did he realize that you don't tempt the gods with that kind of talk. Milton's wife Peggy died of lung cancer two years to the day after the public offering. Eighteen months later, Alan pulled off a coup, ousting his father from the business he'd founded. Humiliated, alone, and depressed, Milton died a few months later.

"What about that trust?" Benny asked.

"There's a sad irony to that timing."

"How so?"

"A month after his wife's death but before his son's coup, Milton set up the Peggy R. Blumenthal Trust. He created that trust for the benefit of all three of his children and he designated himself as the trustee. All well and good."

"But?"

"But he named his son, Alan, as the successor trustee upon his death."

I explained that the trust invested the son, as successor trustee, with just enough discretion to give him grounds, albeit shaky, to refuse to make any distributions to his two sisters.

We ate for a while in silence, and then I said, "He took more than just his father's company."

"What else?"

"Not what, but who. His father's trusted secretary. Her name was Jennifer O'Keefe back then. Apparently, Alan was having a secret affair with her while she was still working for his father and Alan was still married. The rumors are that she helped him gather material against his father as part of the takeover of the company."

"What kind of material?"

"A hodgepodge of emails, notes, phone logs, confidential memos. Just enough for Alan to concoct an argument that his father was no longer competent to lead the company."

"Where is she now?"

"She's still at the company, although she's now a vice president."

"In charge of what?"

"Not clear. Her title has something to do with social media and the company's website. But it sounds like she's basically Isaiah's chief of staff."

"She still shtupping him?"

"Apparently so."

"Is he married?"

"No. Divorced."

"Kids?"

"No."

"You said her name was Jennifer something-or-other back then? Did she change it?"

"She did. She's now Anna."

"Same last name?"

"No last name. At least none in the company directory."

"Just Anna?"

"Yep." I rolled my eyes. "Just Anna."

Benny frowned. "What the hell?"

"I know. I did a little research on the Internet."

"And?"

"And it gets even weirder. Anna was a prophetess, like the Prophet Isaiah."

Benny put down his chopsticks and squinted at me. "You think?"

"I have no idea. This is above my pay grade."

"So what's the deal with his sisters?" Benny took a sip of his beer. "Why's he being such a dick?"

"Maybe revenge."

"Revenge? For what?"

"That family is a mess. His sisters were close with their father. Very close. As were his sisters' kids. He was the beloved Zayde Milt to the grandkids. So you can imagine how outraged Megan and Holly were when their brother took over the company and kicked their father out. The older sister—Megan—posted this angry tirade on Facebook that went viral. I found it last night." I shook my head. "Quite a rant."

"Tell me."

"She calls him a monster—a selfish, arrogant, narcissistic monster. She goes on and on about how he destroyed their father and stole his company. She labels him a psychopath and criminal. Well, once that Facebook post went viral, the media descended on all three of them. Talk about your perfect storm. A TV crew found Megan and Holly at the nursing home with their father. Three other TV crews and several reporters confronted their brother as he was leaving his private lunch club."

"Holy shit. How did that play out?"

"Not good for the future Isaiah. You can find both videos on YouTube. In the nursing home video Holly starts crying over what had happened to her father, who looks a wreck. He would die less than a week later. Meanwhile, outside the lunch club Alan gets forced into an impromptu press conference where he tries to justify what he did to his father."

"Give me a fucking break. Justify?"

"Yep. Claimed he was merely fulfilling his sacred obligations to the shareholders and their equity."

"What a jackass."

"That was definitely the consensus on social media. He got totally scorched. All of which probably explains his handling of that trust fund."

"Explains maybe, but doesn't justify."

"Absolutely. His feelings toward his sisters are irrelevant to his fiduciary duties as the trustee of the trust fund."

"What about his company. Is it still publicly held?"

"Not anymore. He took it private three years ago."

"Why?"

"Interesting question. The public reason is some version of rewarding loyal shareholders. But the real reasons can be harder to pin down. I found an article on the transaction in *Bloomberg* that mentioned his obsession with privacy. If true, that could be a good enough reason for someone who already owned almost half of the company's stock. After all, if you are the CEO of a public company, you're the public face of that company. Nowhere to hide, as he quickly discovered after that Facebook post. Take the company private and you can disappear, which is pretty much what he's done. I did a Google search for him. No newspaper or other media mention in the past two years. He'd changed his name to Isaiah by the time he took the company private."

"But even a delusional, arrogant jerk has to answer to a board of directors, right? What do they say?"

"Come on, Benny. You know as well as I do that the best way to neuter a board of directors is by earning profits, and MP Enterprises is rumored to be one of the most profitable companies in Missouri. I hear every one of those subsidiaries is making money."

Dipping my chopsticks into the soup, I slurped some noodles and cilantro.

"Actually," I said, "there could have been a related reason to take the company private."

"Oh?"

"I spent a mind-numbing afternoon yesterday reading through the last few years of the public company's SEC filings before it went private."

"Ugh."

"Exactly." I set down my chopsticks. "But buried in all those dense footnotes were two intriguing references to Alan—one during the last year he was the company's general counsel and the other a year after he took over the company and ousted his father."

Benny was grinning. "Define 'intriguing.'"

"The footnote text was in that opaque legal gobbledygook that security lawyers have perfected, but both were disclosures of claims of inappropriate conduct by the unnamed general counsel, who was Alan at the time, and later by the unnamed CEO, who by then was Alan."

"Holy shit? Sexual harassment?"

"That's my interpretation of those disclosures. The claimants were both identified as female employees. Unnamed, of course. This was years before the #MeToo movement, and both claims were quietly resolved. But even back then, if either of those women had gone public with their claim, the blowback could have forced him to resign."

"Some prophet." Benny snorted. "What a fucking hypocrite."

"True, but also another reason for him to take the company private."

"Think he's still got a zipper problem?"

"Don't know the answer to that one."

"Could be valuable intel."

"Maybe."

He took a sip of beer. "So what's next?"

I smiled. "I'm meeting with the Prophet tomorrow."

Benny's eyes widened. "No shit? How'd that happen?"

"I sent him a demand letter last Monday. Told him I'd file suit if he didn't promptly comply with his fiduciary duties. Specifically, I told him he had to promptly authorize the last three disbursement requests by each of his sisters, and then he had to appoint as a successor trustee a bank to be approved by the sisters."

"And?"

"Next morning, I receive a phone call from the man his sisters call the Weasel."

"The Weasel, eh?" Benny chuckled. "And who is this Weasel?"

"His name is Arnold Bell. His official title is senior aide to the Chairman."

"Ah, yes. And his unofficial title is Butt Boy in Chief."

"So I hear."

"And what did this Weasel have to say?"

"That 'the Chairman' requests my presence at a private meeting of the two of us."

"The Chairman. That's what he called him?"

"Yep."

"And your response?"

"I explained that it made more sense for me to meet with the Chairman's attorney. That's when I learned that the Chairman has a law degree and had formerly been the company's general counsel. Because this is not a company matter, the Weasel explained, the company's general counsel will not be involved. The Chairman will represent himself."

"Tomorrow morning, eh?"

I nodded. "Ten o'clock."

"Just you and Isaiah?"

"Apparently."

Benny was grinning. "Where can I buy a ticket?"

I sighed. "I'll give you mine for this afternoon."

"What's this afternoon?"

"Another version of bad for the Jews."

"Oy, you mean your Motel."

I frowned. "My who?"

"Motel Kamzoil."

"Who is that?"

"Huh? Who is that? You don't remember Motel? From *Fiddler on the Roof*?"

"No."

"Oy, Rachel." Benny leaned back, placing his hand over his heart. "I am shocked. Rachel Gold, aka the Jewish Goddess of St. Louis, possessor of an All-World Tush, doesn't know the name of the poor tailor from *Fiddler on the Roof*?" Benny shook his head. "Now that is what I call bad for the Jews."

I couldn't help but laugh. "Okay. You said *my* Motel? I still have no idea who you're talking about."

"I'm talking about your client—that Yid tailor."

"Not tailor, Benny. Eli is a dressmaker."

"Dressmaker, shmessmaker—so what's going on this afternoon?"

"We have a status conference before the judge, and probably another settlement offer before that."

"Good. Tell Motel to settle. Tell him it's enough already."

"I've tried, Benny. For him it's a matter of principle."

"Oh, really? As a wise man once said, 'When somebody tells you it's not about the money but the principle, it's about the money.'"

"Not here, Benny. Eli views what happened to him as blood libel. He claims she insulted the entire Jewish people. He says he wants his day in court."

"*Oy.* His day in court? Tell him this isn't a TV courtroom drama where good wins out over evil. He's in the fucking Circuit Court of the City of St. Louis—a venue where shit happens every day."

"I've explained all of that to him, but he's firm. And let's not forget, he's entitled to be firm. That's what lawyers are for."

"Good luck, kiddo—with Motel the Tailor this afternoon and tomorrow with that creepy Prophet."

I smiled. "Thanks."

Chapter Three

I walked Eli Contini into the hallway outside the courtroom
and waited for the door to swing shut behind us.

My voice lowered, I said, "They have a final settlement proposal."

My white-haired client straightened warily, his thumb and
forefinger stroking his goatee. "Now what?"

I peered through the window of the courtroom door. Cissy
Robb and Howard Milton Brenner were huddled in conversation
near the empty jury box.

I turned back to Eli. As always, my slender seventy-three-year-
old client was elegantly attired and perfectly coiffed, right down
to his manicured fingernails. Today's outfit included a light-gray
two-piece wool-silk suit with a white silk pocket square, a starched
white dress shirt, an aqua-and-gray-striped silk tie, and polished
tan wingtips. Though he was perhaps an inch or two shorter
than me, his sharp features and stern demeanor gave him a much
larger persona.

I leaned in close. "You're not going to like it."

He crossed his arms over his chest, his face grim. "I am not a
child, Miss Gold. Tell me."

I took a deep breath. "Cissy will drop the lawsuit if you give
her five designer dresses and a formal letter of apology."

He stiffened, eyes ablaze. "Never. That woman is nothing but a common thief!"

His face red, he raised his right hand, pointing his index finger toward heaven. "Eli Contini apologize to that *nafka*?" He shook his head, chin thrust forward. "As God is my witness, never!"

Several heads turned to stare at my client.

I doubted whether any recognized him, but many sensed that they should, that they were in the presence of a personage, perhaps an Italian duke. Although Eli Contini did indeed trace his lineage back to Venice, his grandfather had been not a duke but a tailor—and a poor one at that, eking out a living in the Jewish ghetto. In the late 1930s, terrified by the rise of fascism and anti-Semitism, Yitzhak Contini brought his young family to America, eventually settling in St. Louis.

Despite those humble origins, the grandson of Yitzhak Contini had risen to aristocracy within the fashion world of St. Louis. He was, after all, the Eli of Eli's on Maryland, which sat at the apex of the fashion world of our town. For decades and countless weddings, debutante formals, and charitable balls, Eli had tailored and clothed the grandmothers, wives, and daughters of the St. Louis ruling class.

"I understand your feelings, Eli." I looked around to make sure no one from the other side was near. "But the cost of five dresses is much less than the cost of a trial. You can end the case now, eliminate your risk, and actually save money."

"Money? How many times do I have to remind you, Rachel? This is more important than money. That woman has violated my honor, and she has violated the honor of my people. This is blood libel. She, not I, is the one guilty of slander. In the Talmud, Rachel, it is said that he who speaks slander has no portion in the world to come."

"Let's first worry about this world." I lowered my voice. "Their case has problems, but it's hard to predict what a jury will do. If you lose, Eli, there could be a big verdict. Her numbers are ridiculous, but we know her lawyer is going to ask the jury for a million dollars in actual damages and another million in punitive damages."

"And you're going to tell that jury that all I ask for is justice." He shook his patrician head gravely. "I am an American citizen, Rachel. I understand my constitutional rights. I chose to exercise them here. I demand my day in court."

I studied him a moment and then gave his arm an affectionate squeeze. "Okay, boss."

———

Cissy Robb and Howard Brenner looked over as we entered the courtroom.

I turned to my client. "Please wait over there, Eli." I pointed toward the rows of benches in the gallery.

Brenner leaned toward his client and whispered something as he gestured toward the opposite side of the gallery.

At forty-one, Cissy Robb was a striking figure with an aura that seemed almost regal. And with good reason. After her husband struck it rich, according to my sources, whatever nature had omitted Cissy set off to acquire from an A-list of professionals in the fields of plastic surgery, orthodonture, personal fitness, hair and makeup, and fashion. As she took her seat in the front row of the gallery, she glanced over at me with what I assumed she believed was an intimidating scowl.

Brenner approached with a hearty smile. He was a stocky man in his early sixties with a ruddy complexion, a shock of gray hair, crinkly blue eyes, and a crooked smile that displayed tobacco-stained teeth. Ironically, Brenner had made a name for himself defending media defendants in libel cases. Today, though, it wouldn't have mattered if he'd been on retainer as special libel counsel to the *New York Times*. That was because Cissy Robb happened to be the wife of Richie Robb, who happened to be the founder and CEO of Pacific Rim Industries, which happened to account for nearly a third of the annual billings of the law firm of Harding Brandt LLC. Although Harding Brandt LLC might trace its origins and carefully burnished image back to the genteel professionalism of the early 1900s, that was then, and this is now. When the wife of your biggest client is unhappy, your job is to make her happy, and if that means making Howard Brenner don the costume of plaintiff's libel shark, so be it. The business of modern law is, after all, business.

"Well, counselor," Brenner said with hearty good cheer, "do we have a deal?"

I shook my head. "Nope."

He frowned. "Jesus, Rachel, does your client understand his exposure here?"

"Last time I checked the case law, Howard, including one appellate case where you represented the *Post-Dispatch*, truth is a complete defense."

He tugged at the loose skin on his neck, his lips pursed.

I said nothing.

He gave me a grudging chuckle. "You drive a hard bargain, Rachel Gold. What's your counteroffer? I probably can whittle my client a couple dresses."

"No counter, Howard. Let's go see the judge."

———

The Honorable LaDonna Williams leaned back in her chair and stared down at her desk with a scowl. In her late forties, Judge Williams had been on the bench for just two years, having previously served for almost two decades in the city prosecutor's office, where she'd been a respected, hard-working attorney. During those years, she'd been a guiding force of the Mound City Bar Association, our local association of black attorneys. Judge Williams was a plump woman with a gentle smile and soft features that masked an incisive legal mind and a no-nonsense courtroom demeanor.

She looked up, leveling her gaze at me. "Now let me see if I have this straight, counselor. Mrs. Robb bought a dress from your client. Correct?"

"Yes, Your Honor. An Oscar de la Renta gown that Mr. Contini specially fitted for her. The total price was over ten thousand dollars."

"But when she attempted to return that dress to your client, he refused to take it back. Correct?"

"That is correct, Your Honor."

"The reason being?"

"Mr. Contini examined the dress and concluded that it had been worn."

Judge Williams turned to my opponent with a frown. "And how exactly does that incident metamorphose into a libel claim, Mr. Brenner?"

Brenner chuckled. "Very simple, Judge. If you will allow me to explain."

Judge Williams rolled her eyes. "I just *asked* you to explain, Mr. Brenner."

"Ah, yes, you are correct. Heh, heh, heh. Well, when the defendant refused to take back the dress, there ensued an exchange of heated words. Or, more precisely, he subjected my client to a barrage of heated—indeed—incendiary accusations."

Brenner attempted to look indignant as he shook his head. "He accused my client of fraud. He accused her of dishonesty. He even accused her...of theft. These scandalous and defamatory charges were overheard by three other women in the store, all of whom knew my client on a social basis. Even worse, two are members of the same country club to which my client's application has been pending. You can only imagine how reports of that incident spread through the country club."

He paused and placed his hand over his heart. "Mr. Contini's false, defamatory, and malicious verbal assault has tarnished my client's reputation, and her reputation is her most precious asset, her most treasured—"

"Counsel," Judge Williams interrupted, "save the violins for the jury." She turned to me. "Fraud and theft? Those are harsh words from your client."

"He was furious at the time, Your Honor. When he refused to take back the dress, Mrs. Robb called him, and I quote, 'a dirty money-grubbing Jew.'"

She raised her eyebrows and leaned back in her chair. "Oh, my."

I nodded. "Your Honor, those were the worst possible words she could have chosen. My client is fervently opposed to any form of anti-Semitism. He's obsessed by it, and with good reason. He lost many relatives in the Holocaust, including two grandparents and two uncles, and he blames those deaths on lies about the Jewish people spread by Hitler and others."

The judge turned to Brenner with a puzzled look. "Not that it's relevant, Mr. Brenner, but isn't your client Jewish?"

"She is, Your Honor." Brenner gave the judge a smile that more closely resembled a grimace. "However, I would point out to the Court that her alleged words are *not* at issue in the case."

Brenner turned to me. "As Ms. Gold can confirm, the defendant has asserted no counterclaim for libel."

"That's because Mr. Contini refuses to stoop to your client's level."

"Whatever the reason, Your Honor, we will be filing a motion to exclude any testimony on that subject."

The judge looked at Brenner, and then at me. "Settlement prospects, counselor?"

I glanced over at Brenner and then back at the judge. "We have two stubborn litigants who believe that what's at stake here is their honor."

"Honor." The judge rolled her eyes. "That's what makes lawyers rich. Well, let's pick a trial date, folks." She opened her calendar. "Perhaps sometime next summer. This is on the jury docket, correct?"

"Judge," Brenner said, "our first priority is to get this case to trial. My client needs to clear her name as soon as possible. If that means waiving a jury, so be it."

Judge Williams turned to me. "Rachel?"

I did my best to pretend to ponder the question. Libel plaintiffs love juries, and juries tend to love libel plaintiffs. Judge Williams was far more likely than a jury to resist Howard Brenner's closing argument histrionics. Nevertheless, I could see why his client might choose speed over greed. Cissy Robb was an indefatigable social climber. With a net worth north of fifty million dollars, she needed more money far less than she needed to remove this purported blemish from her reputation.

I said, "We're prepared to waive a jury, Your Honor."

"How long will this case take to try?" she asked.

Brenner rubbed his chin. "Oh, two days?"

Judge Williams turned to me. "Rachel?"

"Sounds about right. Maybe three days, but no more than that."

"Three days," the judge repeated as she studied her calendar. "You're in luck. I have an opening four weeks from this Tuesday. The eighteenth of next month. How's that?"

"Well," Brenner stammered, "I suppose that's fine with me, Judge, but I'm sure Miss Gold could use a little more time to get her case ready."

He was right. I could use a lot more time. But I couldn't ignore the hitch in Brenner's voice, which seemed more important than additional time.

"The eighteenth is perfect," I said. "We'll be ready."

"Nine a.m." Judge Williams entered the date on her calendar and looked up with a smile. "I'll see you then."

Out in the hall a somewhat edgy Howard Brenner asked, "Are you going to want to take Cissy's deposition before trial?"

I smiled and shook my head. "What for, Howard? We're already loaded for bear."

Which, of course, we weren't. But bluffing is part of the battle.

Chapter Four

I arrived at the headquarters of MP Enterprises the following morning a few minutes before ten. MP Enterprises is housed in a twelve-story glass-and-steel building in the city of Clayton, a thriving suburb just west of St. Louis. The security measures in the building's lobby exceeded those at most airports. After the metal detector walk-through and the ID check, the security guard called upstairs to confirm my meeting. Then he took my photo, printed it onto an ID badge attached to a lanyard, handed me a plastic card that would open the gate to the elevator bank, and told me that my elevator would be number 4. Elevator 4 opened as I approached. I stepped inside, the doors closed, and the elevator started upward. I noticed there were no floor buttons to push. After a few moments, the elevator slowed to a stop, the doors opened, and I stepped out onto what appeared to be the top floor.

Waiting for me at the elevator was Arnold Bell, aka the Weasel. Although my clients had given him that nickname based on his conniving personality, there were certainly weaselly qualities in his appearance, as well. He had a long pointy nose, prominent ears, dark circles under his eyes, a bushy brown mustache, a receding chin, and a thin comb-over. He was shorter than me and slightly hunched over.

Peering up at me, he said in a high-pitched nasal voice, "You would be Miss Gold?"

"I am."

His short-sleeve white shirt was stuffed into a baggy pair of brown pants belted high on his waist, exposing a few inches of dark argyle socks above his thick-soled brown oxfords. Big feet for such a little man.

"Excellent. This way, please."

He turned and started off at a fast pace, leaning forward, arms swinging, feet splaying outward with each stride. I followed a few steps behind.

We rounded the corner, passing clusters of cubicles on the inside and a row of offices on the outside, most of the occupants bent over computers. At the far end of the hall, standing with her back against the wall, arms crossed over her chest, was a tall, slender blonde in her forties with angular features.

Arnold Bell stopped two steps in front of her, gave her a deferential nod, and stepped to the side.

"Ms. Anna," he said, gesturing toward me, "I present Miss Rachel Gold."

Anna stared back, eyes severe, no warmth in her expression. Presumably, this was her trademark Intimidation Glare. She was dressed in a white blouse, a tight black skirt hemmed above her knees, and stiletto black heels. No ring, no bracelet, no necklace, no earrings. Her straight blond hair was pulled back into a bun just above her neckline.

I forced a friendly smile. "Hello, Anna."

She turned to Arnold. In her heels, she towered over him. "That will be all, Arnold. You are dismissed."

Arnold smiled and leaned forward. "Very good."

He turned to me. "Good day, Miss Gold."

And then he spun away and strode off, arms swinging, feet splaying.

"Follow me." Anna turned and started down the other hallway.

We entered a small conference room—four black mesh office chairs around a square table, a sideboard against the wall held a conference phone and tray of office supplies, including pens, highlighters, paper clips, and yellow Post-It notes. A large window along the back wall had a distant view of the Arch, barely visible beneath dark clouds.

Anna took a seat facing me across the table.

After a moment of silence, I glanced around the room. "Where's your boss? He's late."

She shook her head. "The Chairman is concluding a meeting. A far more important meeting than yours. We will be summoned when he is ready to see you."

"That won't work, Anna. He asked to meet with me—not the other way around. I'm here and I'm ready to see him."

"And he is not ready to see you."

I checked my watch and removed a business card from my purse.

"Here's my card. When he's ready to see me, tell him to call and make an appointment. We meet at my office next time."

I slid the card across the table, stood, and started toward the door.

"Stop!"

I turned. She was standing, her faced flushed.

"How dare you! If you walk out of here, I guarantee you will regret it."

I shrugged. "So be it. *Hasta la vista.*"

And out of the conference room I walked.

I had calmed down by the time I reached the twelfth-floor lobby. I was waiting for an elevator when Arnold Bell called out, "Oh, Miss Gold."

He was trotting toward me, panting.

"What is it?"

He gave me a sheepish grin. "I am pleased to report that the Chairman will now see you."

As I stood there considering my options, there was a *ding* and the elevator door behind me slid open. I turned toward the elevator.

"Oh, Miss Gold! Please don't go! I beg you."

I turned back toward Arnold, who looked panicked.

"They sent me to get you," he said. "The Chairman *ordered* me to bring you. If I don't"—he shook his head. "If I don't do that, well—the Chairman—he'll blame me—he'll—he can be very—"

I gazed at him as the elevator door slid closed behind me.

"Okay, Arnold. Lead the way."

Chapter Five

Arnold Bell paused by the older woman—a secretary, I presumed—seated at the desk outside the door to the corner office.

"Is the Chairman ready, Miss Haddock?"

She looked up from her computer keyboard with a frown, narrowed her eyes, and nodded.

Arnold stepped up to the closed door and knocked twice.

From inside came a muffled grumble.

Arnold opened the door slightly. "Miss Rachel Gold to see you, Chairman."

Another muffled grumble.

"Yes, Chairman." Arnold nodded and turned to me with a smile. "The Chairman will see you now."

He stepped aside as I walked past him and then he closed the door behind me.

I felt as if I'd stepped back in time. The room was large and dimly lit. No artificial lights—just whatever natural light came through the windows on this cloudy morning. There were two lit candles on an enormous mahogany desk, the front panel of which was decorated with elaborate wood carvings of what appeared to be curling ivy vines. Behind the desk, seated on a high-back leather chair, sat the Chairman himself.

Isaiah ben Moishe looked nothing like the Brooks Brothers-attired Alan Blumenthal of yore. In his new incarnation he seemed to have adopted the Hebrew prophet look, right down to the white Middle Eastern robe, although he'd opted for the hipster GQ version of a beard—close-cropped stubble—instead of the shaggy Old Testament version. He had round horn-rimmed glasses and a blue-and-white embroidered kippah on his bald head.

He was frowning at the cell phone in his right hand.

Without looking up, he gestured to the chairs facing his desk. "Take a seat."

As I did I noted that Isaiah's desk and the high-back leather chair were on a platform about six inches above the floor, which meant that anyone seated on the chairs below—such as me—would be forced to look up at the great man.

I smiled as I flashed back to the time Benny and I, as junior associates at Abbott & Windsor, were ushered into a similarly structured office of an arrogant opposing counsel in his fifties.

"That's some platform, dude," Benny had told him. "Sorry about your penis."

That meeting did not go well.

"Dammit." Isaiah leaned forward and pushed a button on his desk phone.

"Yes, Chairman," said a woman's voice over the speaker.

"My cell phone issue has not been resolved. This is unacceptable."

"Oh, I am so sorry, sir. I will call Mr. Flynn in IT."

"Forget that bozo. Arnold can handle this. Tell him I will be free in"—he paused to look at me—"in twenty minutes. Tell him he better have his sorry little behind here by then."

"Yes, sir."

"More coffee, Mildred." He glanced at me. "Would you care for any?"

I shook my head.

"Just for me, Mildred."

He pressed the button to disconnect the call, leaned back in his chair, and scrutinized me as he stroked his beard.

"Well?" he finally said.

"That's my question."

He frowned. "Pardon?"

"You were the one who requested this meeting. Thus my question: Well?"

There were three quick raps on the door.

"Come in, Mildred."

His secretary hurried in, carrying a large stainless-steel coffee mug with a black lid. She set the mug on his desk, turned, and hurried out of the room. All the while he kept his gaze on me, not acknowledging her presence.

"Your claims are without merit." He paused to remove the lid from the coffee mug. "That is what you and my conniving sisters will discover if you are foolish enough to continue with your groundless claim. They are a pair of losers, as is anyone stupid enough to associate with them."

"How about we cut to chase, Alan?"

"Isaiah." He took a sip of coffee. "I am no longer Alan."

"Why did you ask for this meeting?"

"You must not have been listening. I just told you why."

"I doubt that. If that was your message, you could have told me over the phone. We both have more productive things to do with our time than participate in this foolish charade."

"This is no charade, lady."

"You want foolish, Isaiah, I'll tell you foolish. If you force me to file the lawsuit, you will spend far more in legal fees than the total of the distributions your sisters have requested to date. And that assumes you don't lose. If you do lose, the court will terminate your position as trustee and you will have the pleasure of paying my legal fees as well as your own. That is what I call foolish."

"And that," he said, his voice rising, "is what I call a matter of principle."

I couldn't help but smile, recalling Benny's quote about money and principle.

Isaiah leaned forward, giving me an Old Testament look of outrage as he pointed his index finger toward the ceiling. "Heed these words. I am a man of principle. I will bend to no man—and certainly to no woman."

I stood and gazed down at him. "Be careful what you wish for. To quote that old proverb, the bigger they are the harder they fall. See you in court, Alan."

And I left his office.

Chapter Six

"Holly Goodman?" Abe said. "I know her."

"A patient?"

He smiled. "She is."

Abe Rosen and I were having our regular Saturday morning *kaffeeklatsch* at Osage Café in the Central West End while our kids—my son, Sam, and his daughters, Sofia and Madeline—were at religious school at Central Reform Congregation. I'd ordered a blue corn biscuit with my latte, and Abe had the goat cheese omelet with his coffee.

We met three months ago, compliments of my mother. Abe had recently moved from Cincinnati to join the OB-GYN practice of Max Kaminsky, my mother's gynecologist and the doctor who'd delivered my little sister and me.

Abe was, in my mother's opinion, the perfect match for her elder daughter: a nice Jewish doctor. And single. As I would later learn, Abe's ex-wife had moved back to her hometown of St. Louis after their divorce to be closer to her parents, and Abe had followed to live closer to his daughters.

But back to my mother the matchmaker. I still remember that moment when she unveiled her grand plan. She dropped by my office after her appointment with Dr. Kaminsky, the high point of which, she announced, was her doctor's observation that she had the uterus of a forty-year-old.

"Not too shabby, eh?"

I congratulated her, at which point she leaned back in her chair, held out her arms, raised her eyebrows, and announced that her uterus was not why she came to my office. No, the real reason was Abe Rosen.

I frowned. "Who's that?"

"Who's that? I'll tell you who's that. A nice Jewish boy, that's who. Better yet, a nice Jewish doctor. And even better, a nice unmarried Jewish doctor. He just joined Dr. Max's practice."

"Okay," I said, growing more uneasy by the moment. "And?"

"And?" I frowned. "And what?"

"And guess who's coming to dinner tomorrow night?"

"Oh, my God, Mom. You didn't."

"I did. I told him I'd make him a nice brisket and my special chocolate babka."

"He's coming to dinner?"

"He certainly is."

"He's coming to dinner at my house?"

"At seven thirty tomorrow, sweetie. After Sam is in bed. But don't worry. I'm taking care of dinner. Everything from soup to nuts. You'll be a guest."

I plopped down in my chair. "I cannot believe this."

"Oh, you're going to like Doctor Abe, Rachel. I guarantee you."

She was right.

I confess, however, that with a name like Abe Rosen, my expectations were low. Abe Rosen sounded like a character in the play *Old Jews Telling Jokes*. A younger version of an old Jew, perhaps, and probably not telling jokes. More like one of those intense pre-med types from college. As the doorbell rang that night, I flashed back to Harold Mishken from my senior year of high school—five foot three, already balding, eyes blurred behind the thick lenses of his black horn-rimmed glasses.

But the Abe Rosen that arrived for dinner that night was not the Abe Rosen I was expecting. Not even close. The real Abe Rosen was tall—almost six foot four. He was trim and athletic— he'd played varsity basketball at Miami of Ohio. He was blonde with hazel eyes. And handsome. Hollywood handsome. Maybe not leading-man handsome, but sexy sidekick handsome. And sweet and intelligent and, as if I'd ordered him from a catalogue, a Jane Austen fan. Yes, Jane Austen.

That was three months ago.

We'd hit it off that first night but then decided to take things slow. Abe's divorce had been final for less than six months, and my life—with my son, Sam, and my two stepdaughters and my law practice—left little room for a passionate love affair. Or at least that's what I told myself. I still had trouble with the image of little Sam climbing into bed to snuggle with me—as he still did a few times a week—and discovering that his mommy was already snuggled with someone else. Not that he didn't like Abe, because he certainly did. And he loved Abe's two daughters. But, so far, we'd keep things rated G, with an occasional PG-13 moment. Which is not to say that I haven't had some X-rated fantasies starring Abe—and that I was becoming more tempted to make them real. For now, though, we kept to our Saturday *kaffeeklatsches* and our occasional family dinners and picnics with all three kids.

"Something's wrong," Abe said.

"What do you mean?"

"You're not yourself, Rachel. Is it one of your cases?"

I took a deep breath and exhaled. "I wish. No, it's not a case."

"Then what is it?"

"You heard about the horrible death of that woman last weekend? The mother of three?"

Abe winced. "Oh, the falling tree in that storm?"

I nodded.

The prior Saturday evening, during a violent thunderstorm, the young mother had run out to the backyard to bring in their dog. A bolt of lightning split a tree, and a huge branch crashed onto her. By the time the ambulance reached the hospital, she was dead.

"Her youngest daughter goes to Sam's school. Her name is Jenny."

"Does Sam know her?"

"Probably not before this. She's two years older. But he knows her now. Everyone in the school knows Jenny now, poor thing."

"Is the school doing anything?"

"They're trying. They've had counselors meet with each of the classes, talking to the kids, that sort of thing."

"And?"

I shrugged. "I suppose it helps some. I've talked with Sam. We talk about it every day. But last night, as I tucked him into bed he asked me a question I couldn't answer. He asked me why God was so mean. I didn't understand. I asked him what he meant. He said, 'Why would God let that that tree kill Jenny's mother?'"

"What did you say?"

I could feel my eyes watering. I took a breath and exhaled. "I told him the truth." I stared down at the table. "I told him I didn't know why God let that happen."

Abe reached across the table and took one of my hands in both of his. After a moment, he said, "None of us do, Rachel."

"I know that. But it's not much of an answer to your child, especially in a world where terrible things happen to good people and good things happen to terrible people. Think of your dad. And my Jonathan. And Jonathan's first wife. And on and on, including most of my mother's family in the Holocaust."

Abe's father had died of a heart attack during the summer after Abe graduated from high school and just a few weeks after his father had joyfully and proudly bought season tickets to the home basketball games at Miami of Ohio, where his son was going on a basketball scholarship. He'd even made his son a blown-up copy of the seating chart at the basketball arena and placed a red circle around his seat so that Abe would know exactly where his dad would be sitting for each home game. And all four years, Abe would look over to that empty seat at least once every home game.

As for my late husband, Jonathan, and his first wife, Robin, she died of ovarian cancer at the age of thirty-four, leaving behind two young daughters. Jonathan died ten years later at the age of forty-four. He'd been determined to get home from a two-week trial in Tulsa in time for our wedding anniversary. Rather than wait for the next commercial flight, which included a change of planes in Kansas City and a one-hour layover that wouldn't get him home until eleven that night, he'd hitched a ride on his client's corporate jet, which took off in a thunderstorm and crashed ten miles east in an oilfield, killing all aboard.

I used the napkin to wipe my eyes. "I need a genuine answer for my son, Abe. And for me."

Chapter Seven

"So what was his answer?" Benny asked.

We were in my kitchen after dinner. I was washing the dishes, Benny was drying, and my mother was upstairs reading a bedtime story to Sam.

I handed Benny a plate. "I'll give him credit. He's thought a lot about it. In addition to losing his dad, his best friend from college died in the World Trade Center on 9/11."

"Okay," Benny said, "but what was his answer?"

"That you can't blame God. That bad things to happen to good people because of bad luck, bad people, or simply the consequences of being mortal in a world of natural laws."

Benny shook his head. "That's it? That's his answer?"

"Pretty much." I shrugged. "Abe's view is that tragedies are not punishments from on high for bad behavior and that they aren't part of some grand design by God. There is no grand design. Abe feels you shouldn't blame God because God had nothing to do with it. Abe's view is that you pray because God is just as hurt and outraged as you are."

Benny shook his head. "So his God is—what?—a New Age therapist?"

"Sort of. I think it helps Abe make sense of things, but"—I

shook my head—"it sure doesn't help me answer Sam's question."

"I'll tell you what else doesn't. When my dad died of cancer, my Rabbi—the great Isadore Silver—encouraged me to read the Book of Job."

"And?"

Benny snorted. "Have you read that crazy story?"

I rinsed a soup bowl as I searched my memory. "I don't think I've read it."

"Then don't. Trust me. That is one fucked-up tale. It's the story of a cosmic wager."

"What do you mean?"

"Exactly what I just said. A cosmic wager. Satan makes a bet with God. Apparently, Job is one of God's darlings—a totally pious dude. Satan tells God that the only reason Job is so pious is because God made him rich and gave him beautiful wives and lots of loving kids. Satan tells God if you were to take away his wealth and kill his wives and kids, Job will turn on a dime and curse you out. 'No way,' says God. 'Way,' says Satan. So God takes the fucking bet and tells Satan to destroy Job's wealth and kill all his wives and kids and his servants."

"Really?"

"Really. I don't know what God's over-under on that bet was, but Satan lost big-time. Job stayed pious. But that's not the worst part."

"Tell me."

"So after God wins the bet, he restores Job's wealth and either brings his wives, kids, and servants back to life or gives him new ones—I wasn't clear on that part. But poor Job is totally baffled. I mean, he must be thinking, 'What is going on here?' So he asks God—he says, 'O Lord, why did you do that to me?' And what does God do? He goes ballistic. 'You think you can understand me,' he roars. 'Where the fuck were you when I laid the foundations of the earth?' Well, that scares the shit out of poor Job, who apologizes for being so presumptuous as to ask God why God had killed all his loving family and destroyed his wealth and made him totally miserable."

Benny shakes his head in disgust. "God's answer? Total B.S. God should have told him the truth. He should have said I made a huge bet on you with Satan, dude, and guess what? I won! I cleaned that jerk's clock."

I handed Benny the soup bowl. "Something tells me that your rabbi may have had a slightly different take on that story."

"No doubt, but I'm not buying it. As far as I'm concerned, the Book of Job confirms my view of the world, namely, that bad shit happens to good people for no reason at all, and if you're looking to God for help, you better hope he isn't on the phone with his bookie."

"Who's on the phone with his bookie?"

We both turned. My mother was at the kitchen door.

"A figure of speech, Mom. How's Sam?"

"What a cutie." She smiled and placed a hand over her heart. "I read him a book, sang him two songs, tucked him in, gave him a kiss, and by the time I got to his door he was sound asleep."

"Oh, that's wonderful. Thanks, Mom."

My mother lives about thirty steps from my back door. More precisely, she lives in the renovated coach house behind my house. After Jonathan died, my mother sold her condo and, God bless her, moved in to help me raise Sam and my two stepdaughters, Leah and Sarah. Leah is now in medical school at Duke and Sarah is a sophomore at Johns Hopkins University.

Although my two stepdaughters call me Rachel, they call my mother Baba, which is Yiddish for grandmother. Their Baba is hardheaded and opinionated and sets lofty standards for her grandchildren. Don't ask the two girls how many times their redheaded Baba made them rewrite their college application essays. Though she can exasperate me like no other human on the face of the earth, we all adore her—and the "we" definitely includes Benny.

Though she recently turned sixty-six, my mother still looks terrific. She works out three days a week in the Fitness Center at the Jewish Community Center—and apparently the arrival of the redheaded Sarah Gold is eagerly anticipated by the older men. They flirt while she's on the Stairmaster and vie for position on the treadmill next to hers. Just last week my mother remarked that there should be a special place in Hell for whoever invented Viagra. I try not to think about the implications of that statement.

The three of us finished cleaning up the kitchen. Benny had an early flight to New York the next morning, so my mother gave him a hug and I walked him to the front door.

"Great dinner, Rachel. Thank your mom."

"I will."

"Hey, speaking of creepy biblical figures, how's that lawsuit against the Prophet Isaiah going?"

"I'll know more after tomorrow. The judge has sent us to mediation. We start in the morning."

"Oh, really?"

"Actually, Isaiah's attorney demanded it, claiming this was a private family matter that needed to be resolved outside of the media spotlight."

Benny chuckled. "I'd say 'spotlight' is an understatement."

"True."

Although I hadn't tipped off any reporters in advance, within hours after I filed the lawsuit I was fielding calls from the local press, and within a day from CNN, MSNBC, and Fox News. Isaiah had initially retained his longtime personal attorney, Calvin Murphy, to represent him in the lawsuit. Murphy was a litigator in his early sixties. He was smart, respected, and mild-mannered. That last quality must have been his downfall, especially after newspapers, television stations, and social media eviscerated whatever seclusion Isaiah may have sought when he took his company private. The lead story in the *St. Louis Post-Dispatch* captured his public relations nightmare in a front-page headline that read: RECLUSIVE MILLIONAIRE ACCUSED OF CALLOUS FINANCIAL ABUSE OF HIS LITTLE SISTERS. Even Rachel Maddow on MSNBC weighed in, using Isaiah (whose new name she found hilarious) as an example of the toxic results of combining power, wealth, and narcissism.

Having suddenly become catnip for the paparazzi, Isaiah decided that he'd rather be represented by someone who could channel some Old Testament wrath and vengeance. Within days after that *Post-Dispatch* headline, Calvin Murphy had been replaced by an outrageous spotlight-loving flamethrower named Gordon "The Hatchet" Hatcher, whose first action was to hold a press conference in which he accused Megan and Holly of "a vile and baseless attempt to embarrass an upstanding citizen through a web of 'fake news.' These allegations," he shouted before a sea of microphones and TV news cameras, "are nothing less than a modern version of blood libel."

Though Hatcher's "blood libel" claim made the evening news, his involvement in the case terminated abruptly two weeks later when the Missouri Supreme Court issued its ruling on a pending disciplinary action arising out of his misbehavior during a deposition where he'd cursed out opposing counsel and then dumped a pitcher of water on him. The Supreme Court suspended his law license, forcing Isaiah to hire his third attorney, a grim divorce lawyer—or, as the lawyers in her field preferred, a "family law lawyer"—named Greta Harding. I say grim because I had yet to see her smile during the two months she'd been on the case. With her brown hair parted in the middle and pulled back into a tight bun, she bore a disturbing resemblance to the farmer's wife in the Grant Wood painting *American Gothic.*

"Do you have a good mediator?" Benny asked.

"I hope so. She's a retired state court judge. Jean Randall. I had a few cases before her over the years. She seems okay."

"Well, good luck tomorrow, kiddo."

"Thanks."

———

I went upstairs, checked on Sam, and came back down to the breakfast room, where my mother had prepared hot tea for us.

In addition to volunteering in the gift shop at the History Museum, she was now tutoring second-graders once a week at an elementary school in the inner city. We talked about those challenges and, more important, the rewards of helping her students get better at reading.

And then she leaned back in her chair. "So?"

I frowned. "So what?"

She gave me one of her knowing smiles. "You and Abe."

"What about me and Abe?"

"Are you two finally *shtupping*?"

"Mom, what kind of question is that?"

"One a mother should ask of her daughter, that's what kind."

I rolled my eyes and shook my head. "Really?"

"Yes, really. I know that a girl shouldn't be opening her legs on a first date but come on now. How long have you two lovebirds been dating? A big virile man like that, well, I shouldn't have to remind you, Rachel, a man's got needs."

"So do I, Mom. But that's not the point. Abe and I are taking this slow. We both agreed."

"Slow for how long?"

"I don't know. We're fine with it. I promise. Okay?"

"Okay, Doll Baby. But remember what that Ecclesiastes fellow said."

"Huh?"

"There's a time for everything under the sun. There's a time to plant and a time to harvest what was planted. Right?"

I gave her a look, "Okay."

"And you know what else? There's a time to meet for a cup of coffee, and then there's a time to say enough already with this coffee."

I shook my head. "Oy."

Chapter Eight

As with most mediations, the morning moved at a sluggish, frustrating pace. Each side sat isolated in its own conference room—occasionally visited by the mediator and, more often, waiting for the mediator to return from the other conference room.

We started promptly at nine. Our mediator, Jean Randall, was a retired state court judge in her seventies. She was short, squat, and squinty-eyed, with a frowning, earnest demeanor. She spent the first hour with us in our conference room diligently exploring different possible settlement options. As I expected, my two clients had different perspectives. Big sister Megan Garber insisted on her brother's total surrender, including dissolution of the trust, distribution of the trust proceeds fifty/fifty to the two women with nothing to the brother, and payment by the brother to each sister of one million dollars for damages caused by his intentional infliction of emotional distress.

Ms. Randall tried to explain to Megan that her settlement proposal was significantly beyond her very best-case scenario at trial, but Megan was not dissuaded. Her sister, Holly, was, however, and I told the mediator that I would discuss the matter in private with my two clients. With a mixture of relief and exasperation, the mediator left us around ten a.m. to go explore settlement possibilities with Isaiah—a task that would no doubt be even more grueling than her session with us.

I explained to Megan that her demands were excessive and that we would need to come up with a far more reasonable proposal if we wanted to trigger serious settlement discussion. Holly agreed with me, Megan disagreed, and that's where we left it at ten thirty to await the return of the mediator.

The mediation was taking place, at Isaiah's insistence, at his company's headquarters. He claimed the mediation had been scheduled on the same day as a potential acquisition of a Spanish company and that he needed to be available if any last-minute deal issues arose. I was fine with that venue. The conference rooms were spacious—and far more luxurious than the one in my office. As were the amenities. As the host of the mediation, Isaiah's company had certain amenity obligations, which, not surprisingly, were delegated to Arnold Bell, who served as our personal butler, bringing hot coffee and cold drinks—soda and iced tea—and when the mediator left to meet with Isaiah and his attorney, fresh pastries and more hot coffee.

It was now close to noon and—other than Arnold Bell's occasional visit to check on coffee, etc.—we'd heard nothing since the mediator left us at ten. I explained to my clients that this pace was not that unusual. I'd been through several mediations where no settlement progress gets made until late in the afternoon. Up until then, it's mostly posturing and killing time.

Megan was standing by the picture window gazing toward downtown, and Holly was seated across the table from me, head down, typing a message on her cell phone.

"I have a question for you two," I said.

Megan turned toward me and Holly looked up with a curious frown.

"It's about your brother."

"Fire away," Megan said.

"I was reading through the annual disclosures the company had to file with the Securities and Exchange Commission. That was back when it was publicly held. If I'm correctly reading the small print in two of those filings, your brother was accused of sexual harassment. Twice. Once when he was still general counsel and the other time when he was CEO."

Megan snorted. "Only twice?"

"That's my question. What do you know—or what have your heard—about your brother and women?"

Megan came over and sat down next to her sister. "Rachel, our brother has always been a sleazebag with women. Don't forget, he was screwing Jenny when he was still married to his first wife."

I frowned. "Jenny?"

"That nasty bitch who was my poor father's secretary—the one who sold him out to Alan. She changed her name to Anna." Megan turned to Holly. "Remember that scandal back in college?"

Holly raised her eyebrows and nodded.

Megan turned to me. "Alan was one of three fraternity brothers who got accused of drugging this poor coed at a fraternity party and raping her."

"Oh, my God. What happened to him?"

"Dad got him a lawyer," Holly said.

"All three had lawyers," Megan said. "Big-time lawyers. They worked out some sort of confidential deal with the university. All hush-hush. I think the fraternity got suspended from campus for a year."

"What about your brother?"

Holly looked at Megan. "Some sort of community service, right?"

"Barely. I think the three guys had to spend a Saturday collecting trash on the campus. Poor girl gets raped and our brother walks away clean."

I shook my head. "That's terrible. What about more recent?"

Megan turned to Holly and raised her eyebrows. "Tell Rachel."

Holly blushed. "I have this girlfriend. She's an assistant manager at the Avalon Apartments. Do you know which property that is?"

"High-rise complex in Clayton, right?"

"That's the one. Purely by accident she found out that our brother rents a one-bedroom apartment there. Except he doesn't rent it under his own name. The tenant is some limited liability company."

"How does she know it's his apartment?"

"She's seen him there."

I smiled. "I guess he's easy to spot in that outfit."

Holly shook her head. "He doesn't wear that outfit when he goes there. The times she spotted him he was wearing jeans, sunglasses, and a baseball hat."

"Was he alone?"

"At least two times, no."

"Who was he with?"

"A woman. And a different one each time."

Megan laughed. "There you go. Our creepy brother has himself a secret fuck pad near his office."

I mulled that over. "I wonder if Anna knows."

"He sure better hope not," Megan said. "That bitch is vicious."

"So I hear."

Just as I looked down at my watch again—it was now ten minutes after noon—there was a knock on the conference room door.

"Come in," I called.

Jean Randall opened the door and peered in. Standing behind her was Isaiah's attorney, the dour Greta Harding, frowning down at her iPhone.

"Yes?" I said.

Ms. Randall forced a squinty smile. "The defendant has an interesting request."

"Let's hear it," I said.

"He wants to meet separately with each of the plaintiffs. One at a time, the older sister first. Just him and her. No lawyers present."

"No lawyers? Really?" I shook my head. "Has he disclosed to you that he is a lawyer?"

"He has, but he promises everything discussed will be strictly confidential. Off the record."

"Has his lawyer agreed to those terms?"

She turned to Greta Harding. "Ms. Harding?"

Harding nodded. "I consent so long as nothing said in that room can ever be used at trial."

"And you, Miss Gold?"

"Let me discuss this with my clients."

"Very well. We will await your answer out here in the hall."

Chapter Nine

"Come in," I called.

Arnold Bell opened the conference room door. "Ms. Garber, correct?"

I nodded as Megan stood.

Arnold smiled at Megan. "Follow me, please."

After they left, Holly turned to me. "But we sued him together. Why shouldn't we talk to him together?"

"It's another instance of your brother's gamesmanship."

"But what's the game?"

"Intimidation, I assume. If he can talk to each of you alone, he thinks he can somehow scare you into settling. That's why I'm glad he asked for your sister first. Even if he hadn't asked, I would have sent her in there first."

"Good thinking, Rachel." Holly giggled. "No one's going to intimidate Megan—least of all her brother."

Indeed, Megan had dressed for the part—blue jeans, a denim Western-style long-sleeve snap shirt, and boots. By contrast, Holly's outfit was more appropriate for a social event at a country club: a navy silk dress, matching low-heeled sandals, and an enormous tan Calvin Klein handbag.

I'd agreed to allow each of my clients to meet privately with their brother on the condition that no settlement could be agreed to without my advice and approval. Not that I anticipated any settlement coming out of those meetings. I didn't need a psychiatrist to diagnose their brother as a spiteful narcissist who had to label any challenger a loser and couldn't stomach the prospect of a compromise. Best-case scenario: what transpired at those meetings could give us insights into their brother's mindset. Thus I instructed both women to listen carefully to everything he said so that they could replay for me as accurately as possible.

And I'd also warned them of their brother's favorite power play, namely, to keep them waiting alone in the conference room. Check your watch when you enter that room, I told them, and if he hasn't appeared after ten minutes, come back to our room.

Holly shook her head. "I really do hate him, Rachel."

"I don't blame you. He's been a total jerk to both of you and, even worse, to your kids."

"I know it's just terrible to say this, but our lives would be so much better if he would just die."

"I understand, Holly. My goal in this lawsuit is to convince the court to give you what you deserve, to sever all financial ties to your brother, and to let him ride off into his own sunset."

We talked mainly about her daughters—or, more precisely, I listened to Holly talk about her daughters. Her elder, Blake, was midway through her junior year of in high school and already caught up in the madness of college preparations—studying for the PSATs, talking with her college guidance counselor, getting recommendations for a writing coach for her application essays. Blake's younger sister, Hayden, was a high school freshman and thus struggling to navigate the treacherous shoals of social life among the mean girls.

After about twenty-five minutes, there was a knock on the conference room door and Megan stepped in, frowning and shaking her head.

"Well?" I asked.

"A total prick." She pulled out a chair, plopped down, looked over at Holly and then back at me, still shaking her head. "Unbelievable."

"How so?"

"First off, he made me wait for what seemed like forever. I was about to walk out when he showed up."

"I'm not surprised."

"The Weasel ushered me into the conference room and said the Chairman was on a phone call but would be in shortly." She snorted. "Shortly. Yeah, right. So he finally walks in. Doesn't apologize. Just starts off quoting some biblical nonsense about empty arguments and viper's eggs hatching and people dying—first in Hebrew, then in English. Made no sense either way. Told me that I needed to repent and ask Hashem for mercy."

"Ask who?" Holly asked.

"Hashem," I explained. "It's a Hebrew word for God. Orthodox Jews use it."

"Whatever." Megan waved her hand dismissively. "I told him to knock it off. I was sick of his bullshit and his showboating. I told him this mediation was his idea, not mine, and that if he wanted to settle the case, Holly and I would need an offer and that it better be a damn good one, too."

I looked up from my notepad. "And?"

"Nothing." She turned to Holly. "He said he wanted to talk to you first. Then he'd tell us how we could resolve the case."

Holly frowned. "Really?"

"That's what he said. I told him that was stupid, that he'd already wasted enough of our time, that if he wanted to settle he needed to come up with a proposal and that his proposal had better include a big fat number."

I said, "Did he ask you how big that number had to be?"

"Nope. He just started quoting some more gibberish from the Bible, gave me some sort of blessing in Hebrew—or at least I think it was a blessing—and asked me to send in Holly."

Holly turned to me. "Should I still go?"

"Might as well get it over with. But remember, Holly: just listen. Don't commit to anything. If he asks you for a dollar amount, tell him you have to check with your sister and your lawyer."

She sighed and started to stand. "Okay."

Megan held up here hand. "Not yet. The Weasel told me he'd come fetch you when his boss was ready. By the way, Sis, did you send him something nasty, maybe by email?"

"Me? No way." Holly sat back down, eyes wide. "Why?"

"He seemed really pissed about—well, it wasn't clear to me—about you sending him some sort of message."

"I didn't send him anything, Megan. I swear."

I leaned over and put my hand on Holly's shoulder. "Ignore it. Sounds like more of your brother's power games."

She turned to me. "Are mediations always like this?"

"Each one is different. The good news for you is that your sister took the brunt."

"Why is that good news?"

I smiled. "Because I don't think it can get any worse."

Famous last words.

Chapter Ten

The first sign of trouble was the distant howl. Barely audible from inside our conference room. Somewhere between a roar and a wail.

Megan looked up from her cell phone. "What was that?"

I stood. "Weird. Sounded like a guy. Your brother?"

I walked over and opened the conference room door. The mediator Jean Randall and Isaiah's lawyer Greta Harding had been seated on upholstered armchairs in the common area between the conference rooms. They were now hurrying down the hall toward the far conference room. Megan and I followed.

Jean Randall pushed open the door, took two steps in, stopped, and leaned back, right hand against her cheek. "Oh, my heavens!"

Greta Harding stepped around her into the conference room. She stared and then spun toward us. "Someone call 9-1-1! We need an ambulance! Now!"

"What's wrong?" a woman's voice called.

I turned. A middle-aged woman—perhaps a secretary—was standing at the far end of the hallway.

"Medical emergency," I called to her. "We need an ambulance."

She nodded, hand over her mouth, and hurried in the opposite direction down the hallway.

Megan had already entered the conference room by the time I turned back. She was standing by Holly, who stood against the far wall, looking down in horror, both hands over her mouth.

I stepped into the room.

Isaiah was curled on his side on the carpet, eyes shut, face contorted, his body twitching every second or two, as if he were having seizures. There was a dark fluid on the carpet near his mouth, some splotched on his beard.

His attorney was kneeling beside him, her hand on his shoulder. "Isaiah? This is Greta. Can you hear me, Isaiah? Isaiah?"

Still kneeling, Greta turned toward Holly with a glare. "What did you do to him?"

Holly's eyes widened. In almost a whisper she said, "Nothing."

"Shut up, Greta." I stepped between them. "Leave her alone."

Someone behind me gasped and uttered, "Oh, my God!"

I turned.

It was Arnold Bell, hand on his forehead, dismayed. "What… oh, my God, what has happened?"

He hurried around me and kneeled next to Isaiah's lawyer.

"Chairman," Arnold pleaded, "where does it hurt? Oh, my goodness, please! Can you tell me, Chairman? Please!"

No response from Isaiah, who had stopped twitching. His eyes were still closed, his face locked in a grimace.

I went over to my clients, who were watching their brother in silence. Isaiah's lawyer and Arnold Bell kept trying to talk to him, trying to get him to respond. Anna entered the conference room and stepped over to Isaiah. She said nothing—simply stood there, hands clenched behind her back, watching as they tried to get a response from Isaiah. His grimace had eased, his mouth was now slack-jawed, and his eyes had opened, but they appeared to be staring at nothing. He gasped, his breath rasping, and gasped again.

"Let us through."

Two EMTs—a tall black man and a stocky Asian woman—entered the conference room with a rolling stretcher. Both were dressed in blue short-sleeve shirts and blue slacks, each with a stethoscope around the neck. Arnold and Greta got out of the way as the woman knelt over Isaiah. After just a few seconds, she turned to her partner.

"We need to go fast."

They lifted Isaiah onto the stretcher on his back, fastened him with two belts, and rolled him down the hall toward the elevator, the two of them almost jogging.

Anna followed behind and, as I would later learn, rode in the back of ambulance to the hospital, where Isaiah Ben Moshe (né Alan Blumenthal) was pronounced dead on arrival.

Chapter Eleven

"That is crazy!" Benny took another sip of beer. "Truly the mediation from hell."

Jacki and Dorian laughed.

"Definitely a first for me," I said.

Benny had dropped by our office for what he described as "a little picnic lunch," which was now spread out on our conference room table. He'd brought a case of STLIPA beer from Urban Chestnut, his three favorite sausages from Volpi (Genoa salame, mortadella, coppa), two slabs of ribs from Pappy's along with huge bag of sweet potato fries, and a sourdough rye bread from Union Loafers. Easily enough to feed ten, though there were just four of us: me, my law partner Jacki Brand, our legal assistant Dorian, and Benny (whose appetite probably brought us closer to ten).

We were gathered one week after the mediation had ended abruptly with Isaiah wheeled down the hall on a stretcher. His burial took place yesterday, having been delayed a few days to permit an autopsy. Apparently, Anna—as his significant other and presumably the executor of his estate—had opposed the autopsy, claiming the delay would violate Orthodox Jewish law, but the medical examiner overruled her objection. As I learned, the medical examiner has authority under Missouri law to order an autopsy when, among other things, a seemingly healthy person dies suddenly. Thus the autopsy before the body was released to the funeral home.

Benny scarfed down a chunk of mortadella, drank some beer, and said, "So what exactly happened in there?"

"Megan had finished her session with her brother," I said, "and come back to our conference room. Other than the fact that he'd been a real jerk to her, Isaiah seemed perfectly healthy. Arnold Bell came to fetch Holly, and she followed him down to the conference room. As with Megan, she had to wait almost ten minutes. Bell told her that Isaiah was in another room taking a phone call."

"Was she alone in there?"

"For the most part. Isaiah's secretary, Mildred Haddock, went into the room to see if she needed anything to drink. She said no. Haddock left. Holly waited. Just her and, on the table, a book in Hebrew and Isaiah's big stainless-steel mug of coffee with the lid. Isaiah came back in the room. No apologies, of course. He stood there, raised that big coffee mug, removed the lid, and took a sip as he stared at her. She said he just stood there for what seemed like forever, glaring down at her and sipping coffee. And then he launched into some scolding lecture about how she and her sister would rue the day they ever sued him, that their girlie lawyer was an amateur way over her head, and that if they had any sense they would settle immediately. He also told her that her threats were pathetic and childish and would only backfire on her and her sister."

"What threats?" Jacki asked.

I shrugged. "Holly says she has no idea what he was referring to."

"So then what?"

I turned to Benny. "When he finished his diatribe, he just stood there, scowling down at her, sipping his coffee, and shaking his head in disapproval. After what seemed like forever, Holly told him that she wouldn't talk to him until he sat down and acted like a gentleman."

"Good for her," Dorian said.

"Did he?" Benny asked.

"Eventually. He sat down across from her at the conference table, still holding the coffee mug in one hand, and slowly shook his head as he stared at her. 'Your turn,' he said. And then it happened."

"What exactly?" Benny asked.

"Holly said it was terrifying. She said he started talking and then stopped. His eyes got wide, he tried to set his coffee mug down but it spilled on the table, he made a painful face, grabbed at his chest or stomach, screamed out in pain, and slid off the chair as he started throwing up. He landed on his side on the ground, groaning and twitching. That's when Holly ran to the door and yelled for help."

"Jeez." Benny shook his head. "A heart attack?"

"Probably, but I guess that's why there was an autopsy."

"What were the results?"

I shrugged. "They haven't released anything yet."

"How are your clients doing?" Benny asked.

"They're still pretty much in shock."

"The good news," Jacki said, "is that his death ends his term as trustee. The two sisters are now the trustees."

"Well," I said, "they will be once we clean up the court case. Anna is his executor, and I doubt she'll be easy to deal with." I turned to Benny. "By the way, Professor, these sausages are amazing."

"Wait 'til you try the ribs—assuming you get one before I eat them all up."

The office phone rang.

Dorian stood. "I'll get it." She left the conference room.

"At least your clients will finally get some of that money they're owed," Benny said.

"I'm hoping we can stay with the current judge," I said, "but we'll probably get sent over to probate court."

Dorian came back in the room, her eyes wide.

"What is it?"

"That was Megan. She's heading down to the police station."

"What for?"

"Her sister Holly. She was arrested."

"Arrested? For what?"

Dorian took a deep breath. "Murder."

Chapter Twelve

By the time I got to the police station, they'd transferred Holly to the county jail. I reached her sister on her cell phone.

"Are you with her, Megan?"

"Yep."

"Tell her I'm on my way over. Tell her not to speak to a soul. No one. If someone tries to interview her, make sure she tells them she's waiting for her lawyer."

"Got it."

"How is she?"

"Freaking out."

"I'm on my way."

When I reached the St. Louis County Justice Center, I stopped off on the second floor to see if a prosecutor had been assigned to the case.

When the receptionist told me his name, I silently groaned. "Is he in?"

"Ah," a familiar baritone voice called from down the hall, "if it isn't the alluring and charming Rachel Gold."

I turned and forced a smile. "Hello, Sterling."

"Such a lovely sight on such a dreary afternoon."

He'd apparently been to the vending machines at the far end

of the hall because he was holding an unopened can of Diet Coke in his left hand. He reached with the other hand to shake mine. We shook.

"What brings you up here, Rachel? Criminal law is not exactly, shall we say, your *métier*."

"Bilingual, eh?"

He chuckled. "*Oui, Mademoiselle.*"

Sterling Walpole was in his fifties. He was tall and trim, with angular features, green eyes, and coiffed salt-and-pepper hair. As usual, he was in one of his dressed-for-success outfits: today's was a Brooks Brothers navy pinstriped suit, a light blue dress shirt, a striped navy-and-burgundy tie, and cordovan wingtip oxfords. You could cast him in one of those law-and-order TV shows in the role of the ambitious prosecutor with an eye toward higher office, which for Walpole was rumored to be Missouri Attorney General—a rumor that seemed to be confirmed by a *Post-Dispatch* story earlier this year reporting that Walpole had recently purchased the domain names WalpoleForMoAG.com and WalpoleForAttorneyGeneral.com.

He frowned. "Oh, my"—he paused, rubbing his chin—"you're here for the little sister, eh?"

"It's your case, right?"

"It is, indeed. Come to my office, Rachel, and we can chat."

I followed him down the hall to the office of the first assistant prosecuting attorney for St. Louis County aka one of smarmiest lawyers in town. I'd twice had the misfortune of being seated next to him at bar association dinners and thus spent most of the evening listening to him bloviate on his favorite topic: Sterling Walpole. Both times I declined his invitation to join him for an after-event cocktail.

Walpole settled behind his metal desk and gestured toward the chair facing him. "Please have a seat, Rachel."

I did.

He opened his can of soda and nodded toward it. "Can I get you something to drink?"

"I'm fine. I don't have much time, Sterling. I'm here to see my client."

"Understood." He chuckled. "Quite a story, eh? A genuine biblical fratricide—the Prophet Isaiah slain by his vengeful sister."

"What do you base that on?"

"The evidence, Rachel. A veritable cornucopia of incrimination. Veritable, indeed. Or, as we learned back in law school, *res ipsa loquitur.*"

"That's a negligence doctrine, Sterling. This is criminal."

He chuckled. "My goodness, I should never attempt to engage in repartee with a beautiful graduate of that esteemed law school along the Charles River."

"You mentioned evidence, Sterling. Such as what?"

"Let's begin with the autopsy, counselor. The results conclusively establish the cause of death. The deceased was poisoned."

"What kind of poison?"

"Cyanide. And guess where else that cyanide was found?" He raised his eyebrows and chuckled. "In the coffee he was drinking at the time of his death. And guess who was alone in that conference room with that large mug of coffee as the victim was concluding an important conference call in the other room? I'll give you a hint: her name, appropriately enough, rhymes with folly."

"That's crazy, Sterling. Where would Holly get cyanide?"

"How about her basement?"

"What are you talking about?"

"We executed on a search warrant this morning. Before we had her arrested. We found two containers of potassium cyanide down there in the lady's basement—one sealed and, alas for you, one opened. And not merely opened. No, clearly some of the contents were gone"

He leaned back in his chair and grinned.

"As the French would say, Rachel, your client *est dans la merde.*"

Chapter Thirteen

"It was horrible, Rachel. I was terrified."

"When did they get there?"

"At five thirty in the morning. I was sound asleep. So were my girls. Suddenly there's this pounding on the front door. As loud as a cannon. I was scared to death. They told me I had to let them in. They said they'd break the door down if I didn't. They said they had a search warrant."

"Did they?"

"I guess. The man in the suit showed me some piece of paper—it looked official." Holly shrugged. "I don't know."

We were in the attorney interview room at the county jail—just Holly and me. Megan had greeted me in the reception area, having exceeded her visiting time limit. She was heading back to her sister's house to see Holly's daughters.

Poor Holly looked the way you would look if you'd been roused from a deep sleep before dawn, stumbled downstairs to find on your front porch a crew of law-enforcement officials armed with a search warrant, then cordoned off with your two daughters in one of their bedrooms during a two-hour search of your home, then given ten minutes to dress before you were hauled off to police headquarters in the back of a squad car where you were booked for homicide, allowed to make one call, transferred to the county jail, and made to don the standard St. Louis County prisoner outfit of a beige cotton top, matching baggy slacks with a tie string, and gray sneakers.

"What did they take from your house?"

"I don't know." She brushed her hair from her face. "When they let me out of the bedroom, there were just two policemen. The others were gone. I don't know what they found or what they took besides my cell phone. They took that, Rachel. My cell phone. I need it. I can't live without it. My God, I have no way to reach anyone."

"I understand, Holly. But you won't be able to get that back unless and until we get you out of here."

"When will you do that, Rachel?"

"I don't know, Holly. They've scheduled the bond hearing for tomorrow. I'll give it my best, but it won't be easy. They've charged you with second-degree murder. Many judges won't grant any bail on those charges."

She slapped her hands down on the table. "I'm going crazy in here." She tilted her head back toward the ceiling. "My God!"

She started sobbing again. I'd brought a little pack of paper tissues with me. There was already a wad of used ones on the table between us.

After a few moments, I placed my hand over one of hers and gave it a gentle squeeze. When she got control of herself again, I told her about the autopsy report.

"I spoke with the prosecutor assigned to the case. He said they found two containers of potassium cyanide powder in your basement. One of those was opened and not entirely full."

Holly frowned. "Cyanide? In my basement?"

I nodded.

"Where in the basement did they find it?"

"He didn't say. I didn't ask. Why?"

"It could have been Marc's stuff."

"What do you mean?"

"Well, technically it wasn't Marc's stuff personally. But after he died, after the jewelry business closed, we hired an auction company to sell off the inventory and supplies. I had them store whatever was left in the basement."

"What kind of things were left?"

"There were jewelry items—mainly some of the cheaper watches and pens and costume jewelry. Stuff like that. There were some tools—like for watch repairs and other kinds of repairs." She frowned in thought. "And yes, I think some of the chemicals he used in the business—like for cleaning gold and stuff. I don't know what kind of chemicals. There were just a bunch of containers—maybe a dozen. I bet that's where they found the cyanide. I wouldn't even know where to buy cyanide. Is it even legal? I mean, if you're not a jeweler?"

"I'll find that out."

I reached across the table and took her other hand in mine. "Holly, I don't know whether I can get you out of here on bail. I'll try. I promise you that. Be strong. I'll come back tomorrow after the hearing and we can talk more."

Chapter Fourteen

"Unbelievable!" Benny shook his head. "They're letting her out?"

"If she can post bail," I said.

"How much?"

"One million dollars."

"A million? I thought she was broke."

"Her sister is the one who'll do the posting." I shrugged. "Hopefully."

"I thought they were both broke."

"They were. But that was while their brother was alive. The trust he managed has more than twelve million dollars in assets. Holly can't access the money herself—at least not for now. Presumably, the prosecution will argue that she killed her brother for the money. But her sister isn't accused of any wrongdoing, and under the trust documents, she is now the sole trustee."

"Megan, right?"

I nodded.

Benny and I were in my conference room. He'd dropped by after his class on his way downtown, where he was to be one of the panelists for an antitrust symposium at St. Louis University Law School.

"How long will it take her to post bond?"

"Good question. You recall the lovely Anna?"

"Isaiah's significant other?"

"Yep. She's already retained a lawyer to fight appointment of Megan as successor trustee."

"Oh, Jeez. Anna? That's all you need."

"Let's just say that no one would confuse the Blumenthal family with the Brady Bunch."

"I can't believe you got that judge to agree to bail."

"I knew we had a shot at it. For starters, she has no criminal record. Not even a traffic ticket—or a parking ticket. And when they brought her into the courtroom, Benny, the very last thing she resembled was a criminal, much less a murderer. Finally, I made sure to remind the judge that she was a widow and the mother of two daughters."

"Who was the judge?"

"Sullivan. Neil Sullivan."

"You got lucky, girl. He's a softy."

"Holly is the one who got lucky."

Judge Sullivan was the former executive director of Legal Services of Eastern Missouri, the local legal aid organization. Unfortunately, he was not likely to be our trial judge.

There was a rap on the conference room door and Jacki Brand stepped in. She held up a large shopping bag. "Brought back some goodies."

"Excellent," I said. "Let's see 'em."

Chapter Fifteen

I gazed at the purse on the conference room table and shook my head in disbelief. "One thousand seven hundred and fifty dollars for that?"

Jacki nodded. "It's a Salvatore Ferragamo. All leather."

"Forget the damn purse," Benny said. "What about the high heels? Who in their right mind would pay nine hundred and twenty dollars for a pair of shoes?"

"Oh, but you have to admit," Jacki cooed, touching one of them lovingly, "these are exquisite."

Jacki had driven to Plaza Frontenac to pick up the materials turned over in response to subpoenas we'd served on Neiman Marcus and La Femme Elegànte. As part of my pretrial preparation for Cissy Robb's libel lawsuit against Eli Contini, I'd obtained a copy of her Visa statement for the crucial month of August. It showed the $10,925.43 charge for the Oscar de la Renta dress that she'd purchased from Eli's On Maryland on August 11 and unsuccessfully attempted to return the following Tuesday. August 11 was a Tuesday. The next day (August 12), according to her Visa statement, she made a $1,750.35 purchase at Neiman Marcus and a $920.67 purchase at La Femme Elegànte. While there were other significant charges on that Visa statement—more than $25,000 in clothing and jewelry alone for that month—what made those two purchases on August 11 and 12 noteworthy were two subsequent entries on August 18: a $1,750.35 credit at Neiman Marcus and a $920.67 credit at La Femme Elegànte. The subpoenas I'd served asked each store to produce the paperwork surrounding the transaction plus the actual items purchased on the 12th and returned on the 18th.

I lifted one of the shoes from La Femme Elegànte. It was a sleek black pump.

"Nice," I said.

Jacki laughed. "It better be. He's my favorite shoe designer."

"Who's he?"

"Who else? Manolo Blahnik."

I looked at Jacki and back at the pump and then back at Jacki. "You amaze me. Last time I checked, I've been a female for at least thirty more years than you yet somehow you know way more about women's fashion than me."

"What can I say? You have a fashionista for a colleague."

"And a hot one, too," Benny said.

Back when we first met, Jacki Brand was a big, beefy Granite City steelworker named Jack Brand who'd quit his day job to pursue his two dreams: to become a lawyer and to become a woman. I hired him/her as my legal assistant at the front end of those pursuits, back when he had just started attending law classes and taking hormone shots and needed my help in picking out appropriate dresses and shoes and a wig. The week after Jacki received her law school diploma, she underwent the surgical procedure to lop off the last evidence of her original gender. When she passed the bar exam, I changed my firm's name to Rachel Gold & Associates, Attorneys at Law. Three years ago, I made her my law partner. Unaware of my plan, she had left for court that morning from the offices of Rachel Gold & Associates. When she returned, the new sign read Gold & Brand, Attorneys at Law. You haven't experienced joy and gratitude until you've been swept off your feet in a bear hug by your blubbering six-foot three-inch two-hundred-fifty-pound high-heeled partner.

I turned over the black pump and studied the sole. There were a few faint scratches around the ball of the foot that suggested, at least to my inexpert eye, that the shoe may have been worn.

"When's this crazy trial start?" Benny asked.

"A week from next Tuesday," Jacki said.

Jacki lifted the Salvatore Ferragamo purse by the straps and stood up, turning to look at her reflection in the window. Although it was a standard-sized black leather bag, against Jacki's bulk it seemed to shrink to a child's play purse.

I gave her an approving nod. "It looks smart."

Jacki gave me a doubtful look.

"You think it'll settle?" Benny asked.

I shook my head. "Neither one is in it for the money."

Still holding the pump, I leaned over and placed it alongside one of my shoes. They seemed the same size.

I looked up at Benny. "It's principle versus status."

"Status? Whose?"

"Hers."

"Hers? Explain."

And so I did.

Eleven years ago, according to a profile I'd read in *Forbes*, Richie Rubenstein was a small-time jobber who'd cornered the U.S. market in cheapo, made-in-Singapore work boots at a time when no one cared about cheapo work boots. Which was fine by Richie. His margins on the schlock he peddled to the inner-city discount stores were just enough to cover the mortgage, the Blues season tickets, and the twice-a-year junkets to Vegas.

But then a miracle occurred: the fickle finger of fashion pointed to work boots. Richie was so far ahead of the curve that it took more than a year for the big players to catch up. With his Asian factories working triple shifts, Richie went from penny ante to pennies from heaven. When a European shoe company acquired Pacific Rim Boots four years ago, his net worth shot from twenty-three thousand to nineteen million dollars.

Richie went berserk that weekend. According to a *Riverfront Times* piece, he chartered a plane and flew his twelve best buds, including the entire bowling team, to Vegas for three days of booze, blackjack, and broads. That same weekend Cissy went uptown. She took the wife of Richie's investment banker to Hilton Head Island and spent three days pumping her for information on St. Louis society. Richie returned with a cosmic hangover and a genital rash of indeterminate origins. Cissy returned with climbing ropes and pitons.

"She's come a long way," I said. "Once upon a time she and Richie were shopping at Walmart, driving an old Chevy station wagon, and celebrating their daughter's *bat mitzvah* with baked mostaccioli and lime Jell-O in the temple basement. She's not backing down."

"So what does she want?" Benny asked.

I slipped off one of my shoes. "Total vindication."

"Vindication from what?"

"On the day of their argument, when Eli called her a fraud and thief, there were other women in the store, including members of the country club she's been trying to join. Even worse, the husband of one of those women is on the club's membership committee. In other words, for her it is definitely not about the money."

"What about your client?" Benny asked.

"Eli is convinced that she bought that dress with the intent of wearing it somewhere and then returning it. He claims she's done it before. When she called him a 'dirty Jew,' he went ballistic. Anti-Semitism is his hot button." I glanced at Jacki. "Right?"

Jacki turned to Benny. "Rachel was stuck in court last week when Mr. Contini showed up for an appointment. I learned all about the Dreyfus Affair in France and the Protocols of the Elders of Zion and the Russian pogroms and the blood libel and his personal hero, Joseph Samuel Bloch."

"Who?" Benny asked.

"I'd never heard of him, either," I said. "He sounds like an amazing guy. Tell him, Jacki."

"Mr. Contini told me that Bloch was a rabbi in Austria in late 1800s. That was not a good time or place to be Jewish. Fifteen Jews were accused of murdering a girl named Esther Solymosi to use her blood to make unleavened bread for the Passover ceremonies."

"What?" Benny said, incredulous.

"The infamous blood libel," I said. "And that was hardly the first time."

"According to Mr. Contini," Jacki explained, "blood libel claims against Jews date back to the twelfth century."

"So what happened to the Jews accused of murdering the girl?" Benny asked.

"This powerful priest—" Jacki turned to me. "What was his name?"

"Father August Rohling. He was a professor at the University of Prague."

"Rohling claimed that he could prove the existence of the blood ritual," Jacki said. "Bloch fought back. He gave speeches and wrote articles. He accused the priest of ignorance and dishonesty. He accused him of willful perjury. Rohling sued him for libel, but Bloch's arguments were so powerful that Rohling dropped his lawsuit and ended up losing his professorship. After the fifteen Jews were freed, Bloch started publishing a newspaper that fought anti-Semitism. Later, he became a member of the Austrian parliament, and eventually he got three powerful Christian men thrown in jail for accusing a group of rabbis of the blood ritual."

Benny raised his eyebrows, impressed. He turned to me. "Cool."

"I agree. Eli sees his fight here as a personal tribute to his hero."

"Okay. But still, can he prove she wore the dress?"

I glanced over at Jacki, who raised her eyebrows and shook her head. I looked back at Benny. "Not yet."

"Excellent. Does the Great Contini understand that he'd better get ready to bend over and kiss his principled *tokhes* good-bye?"

I slipped my foot into the pump. "Well, well. It fits."

I stood up, wobbling on one heel.

Jacki handed me the other one. "Here you go, Cinderella."

I kicked off my other shoe and slipped on the second pump. I did feel a little like Cinderella. I confess I have never owned anything by Manolo Blahnik.

I turned to Jacki. "Do you realize, that this pair of shoes costs more than all of my shoes combined?"

"Nice," Jacki smiled, admiring the shoes. "They're definitely you, Rachel."

I tilted my head back and fluffed my hair in an exaggerated Hollywood pose. "Thank you, dahling."

I took a few sashaying steps and looked back toward Jacki. We both started giggling like school girls. It was a nice respite from the grind of this case.

Benny rolled his eyes heavenward and shook his head. "What the fuck is this? A costume party?"

"Hush, grumpy," I told him.

I returned to my chair and slipped off the heels.

"Are you shitting me, Rachel? The damn trial is less than two weeks away and this is all you got? A couple of returns? She's just gonna say she bought this crap, brought it home, decided she didn't like it, and took it back. Then what are you going to do?"

I put the shoes on my desk and turned to Jacki. "Speaking of which, do you have time this afternoon to do some research on the *Post-Dispatch*'s website?"

"Sure."

"Good. I'm totally jammed. Go on their website and see what you can find for the Saturday of that week. And maybe the Friday and Sunday, too. There's a section in there called 'Style Plus.' They run a column on society events, especially charity fundraisers."

"What am I looking for?" Jacki asked.

"Best-case scenario, Cissy's name. Otherwise, you're looking for every event mentioned and every person identified as attending. Same with the *Ladue News*. They cover all those society events. They take lots of photos, too."

Jacki was jotting down my instructions. When she finished, she looked up with a puzzled expression. "Why?"

"A hunch." I gestured toward the purse and the heels. "In a two-day period, Cissy Robb spent close to twelve thousand dollars on a dress, a pair of shoes, and a purse. The following week, she returns, or tries to return, everything. Maybe Benny's right—maybe she just had second thoughts. But Eli is convinced she wore the dress. If he's right, we have an alternative scenario, namely, that she bought the outfit specifically for an upcoming social event. Given the Visa statement, that would mean that the event had to take place sometime between August twelfth, when she bought the shoes and purse, and August eighteenth, when she returned them and tried to return the dress."

"I like it." Jacki paused, her smile fading. "But..."

"But what?"

"If your hunch is right, why would she risk getting exposed?"

"Good question. Probably because she's rich."

"What do you mean?"

"You know that quote by F. Scott Fitzgerald? About the very rich being different than you and me? I stumbled across it reading a collection of his short stories. It's from the opening paragraph of a story called 'The Rich Boy.' He goes on in that paragraph to explain that the very rich believe, deep in their hearts, that they are better than the rest of us, and thus they get to play by their own rules. That's Cissy Robb—and that's definitely her husband, Richie. I hear he's an arrogant jerk. I wouldn't be surprised if he was the one who told her to return all that stuff."

"You think?" Jacki said.

"Possible. But she's the one who did it."

"If that's true—if she actually wore that dress—why the lawsuit?"

"I've seen this before, Jacki. An arrogant rich person gets in an embarrassing public situation, like her argument with Eli in front of those other women, and the first reaction is inflict pain through an expensive libel lawsuit. More often than not, it backfires. I was in one of these cases back when I was an associate at Abbott & Windsor."

I looked over at Benny. "Remember that Cromwell case?"

Benny laughed. "Oh, yeah. What a douche."

I turned back to Jacki. "Same thing here. Cissy thinks she gets to play by her own rules. She can't. The rules here are the rules that govern the law of defamation. And guess what? One of those rules is that truth is a complete defense."

"Let's hope we can prove it, Rachel," Jacki said.

"I'll check that date with Eli, too. If there was some big event that weekend, maybe some of his other customers mentioned it."

I looked at Benny, who raised his eyebrows skeptically. I smiled and raised my hands. "Well, Professor, you have any better ideas?"

He grunted. "Yeah. Get your client a good bankruptcy lawyer."

Chapter Sixteen

"Little Bear and his mother went home down one side of Blueberry Hill," I read aloud, "eating blueberries all the way, and full of food stored up for next winter."

I glanced down at Sam, who was staring enthralled at the illustration on the page of *Blueberries for Sal*, one of my favorite children's books of all time.

"And Little Sal and her mother," I continued, "went down the other side of Blueberry Hill, picking berries all the way down, and drove home with food to can for next winter—a whole pail of berries and three more besides."

Sam was grinning, no doubt identifying with Little Sal, who'd spent most of the afternoon on Blueberry Hill eating rather than collecting blueberries.

I'd discovered *Blueberries for Sal*, and Robert McCloskey's other gem, *Make Way for Ducklings*, as an adult when I became the stepmother to my late husband Jonathan's two young daughters. Those two illustrated books, along with a treasure trove of others, had filled the girls' bookcase, which was now Sam's bookcase.

Blueberries for Sal—and so many others—were magical, for me and the children. Like his two stepsisters when they were young, Sam could listen to me read them for hours. Each night he got to pick two for bedtime—with the rule that only one could be about trains or trucks. (Tonight it was *Mike Mulligan and His Steam Shovel*.)

I finished the story, leaned over, and gave Sam a gentle kiss on his forehead. "Goodnight, smoochy."

"Goodnight, Mommy."

I turned toward Yadi, who was in his usual bedtime position curled up on the comforter at the foot of Sam's bed. Yadi was our collie-shepherd mix—one straight German shepherd ear, one floppy collie ear, and a gentle temperament unless you were a stranger approaching Sam or me, at which point he morphed into a junkyard attack guard.

I scratched Yadi on the head. "Goodnight, buddy."

He flopped his tail three times and settled his head back down on the comforter.

I paused at the door. Sam was already curled on his side, his arm around Bobo, his stuffed polar bear doll.

"I love you, Sam."

He smiled, his eyes closed.

———

My mother was at the kitchen table, sipping her cup of tea and paging through the printouts from my afternoon of research at the library. She'd dropped by after dinner with a plate of her fresh-baked chocolate rugelach. Sam got to eat two before bedtime, along with a glass of milk. My mother had boiled water for tea while I put Sam to bed.

She looked up when I entered the room.

"Here you go." She gestured toward the teapot, the plate of rugelach, and my teacup, all arranged on the table. "Help yourself, sweetie."

"Thanks, Mom."

"So it's true." She nodded toward the printouts and other papers.

"Yep." I shook my head wearily. "From blueberries for Sal to cyanide for Isaiah."

"And this," she said, again nodding toward the printouts, "this is why it was in her basement."

"That's the best explanation. According to those research materials, cyanide is a fairly common chemical for jewelers. They use it for chemical gilding and buffing. Holly still had all the old records from the store. The invoices show he bought one or two containers of potassium cyanide every year."

My mother leaned back in her chair and smiled. "There you go. Case closed."

"Hardly, Mom."

"What do you mean?"

"All it shows is that there was an innocent reason for why those containers were in Holly's basement."

"Exactly."

"But just because there's an innocent explanation for that poison in her basement doesn't translate into an innocent explanation for the poison in her dead brother. Regardless of how that poison ended up in her basement, the fact remains that it was in her basement, and thus she had access to it."

"What are you saying? That she did poison him?"

"Of course not, Mom. I'm just saying it doesn't help her defense."

My mother frowned as she thought it over. "If she didn't poison him, then whoever did sure wanted to make it look like she did poison him."

"Exactly."

"Which means...which means what?"

"Which means the killer was fairly certain she had a container of cyanide in her basement."

"But how would the killer know that?"

"I suppose the killer could have made an educated guess based on Holly's late husband's business, but then he—or she—would have to have been fairly certain that Holly had those supplies in her basement. Unless…"

"Unless what?"

I frowned. "Unless the killer actually saw those containers in her basement."

"You think the killer was in her basement? Really?"

"Maybe, maybe not. I don't know, Mom."

"And what's this craziness about the text messages?"

"That's a real problem. There were three texts. All sent to Isaiah's cell phone in the days before the mediation. The good news is that they weren't sent from Holly's cell phone. The prosecutor had it searched, and we did as well. No texts to her brother." I paused. "But…"

"But what?"

"They claim she could have used a burner."

"A what?"

"One of those cheap prepaid cell phones. You can buy them at Walmart and Target. They come loaded with minutes and no formal plan. They're apparently popular with some criminals. You use them, throw them away, and no one can trace the phone or the calls or the texts back to you."

"That's what they think she did?"

I nodded.

"They think a nice Jewish girl would know about that burner thing?"

I nodded again.

"That's ridiculous."

"Yes and no."

"What do you mean no?"

"Those three texts were highly personal. Things that only Holly or Megan or their brother would know."

"Such as?"

I reached for the papers and I sorted through them until I found the printout of the texts.

"Here's the first one, sent a little after eight p.m. on June twenty-fourth. That was four days before the mediation. It reads: 'Remember when I caught you wearing Mom's bra and panties? You've always been a total pervert and loser.'"

"Is that true?"

"Holly said it happened. She walked into his bedroom one afternoon—she was about eight, he was twelve—and he was standing in front of the mirror in nothing but a bra and panties."

"Oy, vey! Who else would have known that?"

"No one but her sister, Megan."

"What about the other two texts?"

I looked down at the printout. "In this one—sent the next day at four forty in the afternoon—she said he was always a cheat and thief, and she used the example of when he stole a twenty-dollar bill from their father's wallet and used it to buy firecrackers to light and throw at the dogs in the neighborhood. In the third one—sent to her brother's cell phone the night before the mediation—she said he was an embarrassment to the family and used the example of the time he got drunk and threw up at Megan's *bat mitzvah* party."

"And these things really happened?"

I nodded.

"But she denies sending those messages?"

"She does."

My mother rubbed her chin and stared down at her teacup. She looked up at me and shook her head. "This girl's got some real *tsouris*, Rachela."

"I know."

"So what are you going to do?"

"I don't know."

My mother studied me for a moment and then smiled.

"What?" I said.

"You'll figure it out. One thing you got plenty of is brains."

"I don't know, Mom."

"I know my girl. As your father used to say, 'She's a smart one, Sarah.'" My mother nodded. "You'll figure it out."

I smiled. "To quote Dad, 'From your lips to God's ears.'"

Chapter Seventeen

"What a nasty cunt!"

"She's angry, Megan, and she's in mourning."

Megan shook her head. "No excuse. She's wealthy now, and all because that miserable prick is dead. How much of his stock in that company did she inherit?"

"Her shares are apparently worth at least five million."

Although Anna was not Isaiah's wife and thus not his legal heir, he had apparently designated Anna as the heir of a certain percentage of his shares of stock—a percentage now worth millions.

"And she's angry?" Megan snorted. "Gimme a break. She should be ecstatic."

"Money isn't everything."

"Oh, yeah? Not the way she was acting in there."

Megan and I were in the hallway outside of the courtroom, where the judge had just overruled Anna's objection to the decision of Megan, as her brother's successor trustee of the Peggy R. Blumenthal Trust, to use one million dollars of the trust's funds to post bail for her sister, Holly.

Megan chuckled. "I have to say, Rachel, that was quite a show in there."

I smiled. "And I didn't have to say a word."

"By the way, I think that judge might have the hots for you."

"Not that judge, Megan. But, as you saw in there, he is not fond of blowhards."

Anna had arrived for the hearing with a battalion of five lawyers and two paralegals from the St. Louis office of my old law firm, Abbott & Windsor, which handled most of the legal matters for Isaiah's company, MP Enterprises. But when the clerk called the case and their lead lawyer stepped to the podium, I had to smile.

Yale Rockwell, the silver-haired senior partner, was a terrible choice for that courtroom. Yale is a pompous man whose condescending manner only increases when his adversary is a woman. This made him the worst possible lead counsel before the Honorable Silvio Maccarone, whose judicial temperament seemed to be the consequence of a combination of height (barely five feet), a stutter, a volatile temper, and a last name pronounced the same as the pasta. Little Stuttering Silvio must have suffered plenty of teasing on the middle school playground.

But now, three decades later, perched high on his judicial bench, clad in a black robe, clasping a gavel in his tiny hand, and sneering down at the lawyers below him, the Honorable Silvio Maccarone was ready for revenge. And as he had glared at Yale Rockwell, I could only imagine his flashback to some high school jock making fun of him in the hallway. Having spent his formative years as the victim of bullies, few things enraged Silvio Maccarone more than attorneys attempting to bully other attorneys, especially female attorneys. He was, after all, the youngest (and tiniest) of eight siblings and the only boy—and thus could do little to help any of his older sisters when they were being harassed.

I never got to speak at the hearing. When Rockwell concluded his pretentious oration at the podium, he gestured toward me and said, "I now yield to the young lady lawyer and her unenviable task of trying to overcome our compelling objection."

Judge Maccarone sniffed in disgust.

"Are you serious, counsel?" he demanded in his high-pitched, nasal voice.

Rockwell had paused, leaning back. "Pardon me?"

"An unenviable t-t-t-task? Is that what you called it?"

Rockwell frowned. "I did, indeed."

"Let me ask you something, Mr. Bigtime F-f-f-fancy Lawyer. Did you happen to take a course in t-t-t-rusts in law school?"

"Why, yes. I most certainly did."

"And did you pass?"

Rockwell's face was now flushed red. "Of course, Your Honor."

"Well, you might want to call that professor and ask for a t-t-t-tuition refund because you certainly f-f-f-flunked today." He banged the gavel. "Objection overruled."

The judge turned to me with a smile. "Your client is free to proceed, Miss Gold."

Rockwell stormed out of the courtroom, followed by his pack of legal wolves. Megan and I entered that hallway just in time to hear the end of his rant against that "moronic little piece of dago excrement" as the elevator doors closed.

We sat on one of the benches in the hallway as I explained to Megan the formalities of posting bond.

"Jacki will meet you over there at two this afternoon and walk you through the process. Call her if you're running late."

"Got it."

"I have a crazy day tomorrow. Let's all plan to meet at my office on Saturday morning. Say, at eleven."

"Okay."

"When you take Holly home today, ask her if she remembers any stranger going into her basement in the last year or so."

"Her basement?"

I explained the mystery of the cyanide containers.

"That's weird," Megan said.

"I know. All I can think is that someone else might have seen those containers down there."

"Like who? The cable TV guy?"

"I have no idea, Megan. Maybe no one. But see what she remembers. It could be important."

At that moment the courtroom door swung open and Anna stepped out, followed by her assistant, a short slender young Asian woman. Both were dressed in long black dresses and flats. Neither had any jewelry. Both had their hair—blond for Anna, black for her assistant—pulled back into a bun just above their necklines.

As they started down the hallway, Anna saw us. She stopped in front of the bench and stared at Megan. Her assistant kept her head down.

Megan gazed back at her, defiant. "Yeah?"

Anna shook her head. "You and your nasty sister are cursed."

"Cursed?"

I winced internally. Megan was revving up and there was no way to sidetrack her.

Megan stood, her face flushed. "You want cursed, you bitch? How about this? There's no one left to fuck you but yourself."

I kept a straight face, not attempting to parse that curse.

Anna just stared, first at Megan, then at me. She turned to her assistant. "We are out of here."

I watched them walk down the hall. After they stepped into an elevator, I looked up at Megan with a resigned smile. "We are out of here, too."

Chapter Eighteen

I stopped by the office around five thirty on my way home on Friday. It had been a crazy week—so crazy that Saturday was going to be a workday for me. I had back-to-back meetings scheduled that morning with Eli Contini and then with Megan and Holly. The plan was for me to drop Sam off at the synagogue for his religious school class Saturday morning and for my mother, God bless her, to pick him up after class for lunch. I'd meet them at the restaurant and then we'd take Sam to the zoo.

The office was empty that Friday afternoon, but Jacki had left a nice surprise for me in the center of my desk: a photocopy of the society column from the "Style Plus" section of the Sunday, August 16, edition of the *Post-Dispatch*. She'd circled the middle paragraphs, which described the highlights of the Carousel Auction Gala at the Ritz-Carlton put on by the Friends of the St. Louis Children's Hospital:

> Guests gathered last Friday night under the carousel in the smaller of the two ballrooms at the Ritz, where a bar had been set up in the center with bartenders serving on all four sides. High above the bar and

bathed in spotlights was a slowly rotating carousel, and at each of its four corners was a gilded carousel horse dressed in burgundy and teal blue. Waiters passed silver trays of delicious hot hors d'oeuvres to guests as they signed up for the silent auction items displayed around the room.

Chairwoman Cynthia Barnstable said the event netted more than $900,000, including $350,000 from the auction itself, whose luxury items ranged from a one-week stay in a beachfront mansion along the Costa del Sol to a corporate suite at next year's Super Bowl. Three hundred-fifty guests paid $500 and up for their tickets to the event. The money will be used for the new Neuro-rehabilitation Unit at Children's Hospital.

The article included a photograph of two women standing in front of a carousel horse. The caption identified them as Cynthia Barnstable, chairwoman of the event, and Prudence McReynolds, president of the women's auxiliary of Children's Hospital. The photo credit named Charles Morley.

Jacki had circled Morley's name, drawn an arrow to the margin, and jotted the following note:

> We may have to subpoena this guy, but I'm hoping not. I called him. He agreed to meet for a drink after work at Brennan's. Fill you in later.

Chapter Nineteen

Eli Contini shook his head. "Never, Rachel. I would view it as a betrayal."

Yadi groaned. We both looked over, but he was sound asleep on the rug.

It was Saturday morning. Eli and I were in my office going over a few matters in preparation for the libel trial that was just a little over a week away. After dropping Sam off at the synagogue, I'd gone for a jog through Forest Park with Yadi. We'd stopped by Kaldi's Coffee House afterward for a snack—a blueberry scone and a large coffee for me, a pumpernickel bagel and a small bowl of water for Yadi. Then we drove over to my office, where Yadi promptly fell asleep, front paws over his ears.

Eli and I made quite a Saturday contrast—me in my St. Louis Browns baseball cap (to keep my curly hair out of my face as I jogged), an oversized gray Cardinals sweatshirt, black jogging tights and Nikes; Eli in an elegant navy pinstriped double-breasted suit, white shirt, gold-and-gray-striped tie, and black Italian shoes buffed to a brilliant shine.

"Eli, I can explain to your customers that I got their names from a guest list for the event. They'll never know my real source."

"But I would know, Rachel. A secret betrayal is no less a *shanda* than a public one."

"It's hardly a sin." I tried to hide my frustration. "Three of your customers bought dresses for the Children's Hospital benefit. You said yourself that all three are loyal patrons. If one of those women can remember what Cissy Robb was wearing that night, and if it turns out that it was your dress, I'm sure she'd be happy to help you by testifying at trial."

Another adamant shake of the head. "Out of the question. That woman slandered me and my people. Our people, Rachel. Yours and mine. I would never ask one of my ladies to sully her hands in this coarse dispute. This is my problem and my responsibility. I must force this slanderer to drop her case."

He reached into the breast pocket of his suit, removed the white handkerchief, patted it against his forehead and replaced it, making sure to position it perfectly in the pocket. I leaned back in my chair and tried to hide my emotions. Ten thousand retailers in St. Louis, and I end up representing the Rabbi Bloch of designer dresses.

"Eli," I said patiently, "Cissy Robb has sued you for millions of dollars. She will swear that she never wore that dress."

"But she's a liar."

"We still have to prove it's a lie. Otherwise, she's entitled to a judgment in her favor."

He gave me a serene smile. "Ah, but that will not happen."

"Oh? And why not?"

He made a sweeping gesture with his hands. "Because, my dear Rachel, you will not allow it to happen."

I smiled in resignation. "Eli, my name is Rachel Gold, not Perry Mason. I'm limited to admissible evidence, and, frankly, we could use some more of that."

"But, Rachel, I thought that you found some. What about that fellow from the newspaper—the gentleman who took the photographs?"

"Maybe. We may still serve him with a subpoena, but Jacki met with him last night. She bought him a drink at Brennan's. She told me that he brought along his camera and they went through his photos from the event. Cissy isn't in any of them. He may still have some more on a thumb drive, but I'm not optimistic."

He grimaced. "A pity."

"The *Ladue News* covered the event as well. They included three photos with the article. Cissy isn't in any of them. We're going to try to contact their photographer to see what else she has on her camera."

Eli nodded with satisfaction. "There. You see?"

"Don't get your hopes up." I leaned back and sighed. "I'm not optimistic."

"Oh, but you should be. You are such a lovely young lady, Rachel, and so intelligent. God smiles down upon you, my dear. I am certain you will find us our evidence. And if not, well"—he paused and gave me a shrug—"such is the way of this world. But," he placed his hand over his heart, "you must not chide me for refusing to allow my darling ladies to get dragged into this case."

I rested my chin on my fist and smiled at my courtly white-haired client. "I would never chide you, Eli."

He leaned over and patted my hand. "I promise to be a good witness. It will be her word against mine. That may be the best we can do. We must pray that justice prevails."

I said nothing. My client was in a sentimental mood, and I saw no reason to shake him out of it. I still had a little over a week to come up with something more than a prayer. I had read somewhere that the Prophet Elijah was a miracle worker. We could use certainly use one.

Chapter Twenty

"Our best defense is that you are not a moron."

Holly frowned. "I don't get it."

"Let's say you actually wanted to kill your brother."

"But I didn't."

"But let's pretend, okay?"

Holly glanced over at her sister and then back at me. "Okay."

The three of us were in my conference room. Holly and Megan had arrived just as I was walking Eli Contini out of my firm's offices. The sight of Contini brightened Holly's day. She had clearly been crying on the drive over, as evidenced by her puffy eyes and smudged mascara. Megan was escorting her into the reception area, an arm around her waist, when Holly looked up and immediately recognized Contini.

"Oh, my goodness!" she said, eyes wide and smiling. "Mr. Contini. How are you?"

"I am fine, Mrs. Goodman." He leaned forward and kissed her gently on each cheek. "How are you holding up, my dear?"

"Okay, I guess."

Megan said, "She's hanging in there. Come on, Holly. We can't keep Rachel waiting. Good to see you, sir."

Holly gave Eli Contini a hug and followed Megan into my office.

"So you decide to kill your brother," I continued. "Assuming that you are a rational human being, you'd like to get away with the murder, right?"

Holly frowned and then nodded.

"So let's take this step by step. First, if you wanted to get away with the murder, would it be a good idea to put poison in his coffee when you are the only one in the conference room at the time—indeed, when we've all been told that he is on a conference call and will join you shortly? Of course not. Number two: If you were going to poison him, would it be a good idea to use a form of poison found in your basement? Of course not. And number three: If you were planning to kill him at the mediation, would it be a good idea to send him a few nasty and highly personal text messages during the days leading up to the mediation? Of course not. Unless, of course, you are a moron. And we can all agree, Holly, that you are not a moron."

Megan laughed. "Hear, hear!"

Holly gave me a quizzical look. "So what are saying?"

"I'm saying that the more likely explanation is that someone set you up."

"Who?"

"We don't know—at least not yet—but my guess is that it had to be someone at that company—someone who was able to sneak cyanide into your brother's coffee."

"And," Megan added, "someone who felt fairly confident that you had cyanide in your basement."

Holly shook her head. "But who could that be? No one from that company, including my brother, was ever in my basement."

"My assistant checked your real estate records yesterday. Did you refinance your mortgage about six months ago? Through Mid-State Mortgage?"

"Mid-State Mortgage? Yes, that's the one. But that was after I was turned down by another—oh, my goodness, by one of my brother's companies." She turned to Megan. "What's it called?"

Megan squinted. "I think it's MP Mortgage—or maybe MP Financial. It's one of the MP companies."

"Do you recall why they turned you down?" I asked.

Holly shook her head. "I just got a letter in the mail rejecting my application."

"After you applied for a loan from that company, did they do an inspection?"

"They did—or, no, they had some company do it. Two men, I think."

"Were you there when they came to the house for the inspection?"

"I was. They were there for, well, at least an hour. Probably more."

"I assume they went into the basement."

"They did. And even the attic."

"They took pictures, right?"

Holly's eyes widened. "You're right. They did."

"They usually do. For their report. Were you down in the basement with them?"

"I was. Just one of them went down. I think the other was on the roof."

"The one in the basement. He took pictures?"

She squinted, trying to remember. "He did. Plumbing stuff, water stains, something with the furnace, things like that."

"Do you remember what company they were with?"

She frowned. "I think it was Bates Construction or maybe Bates Contractors. I'm pretty sure about the Bates, just not the rest. I know they gave me some paperwork—maybe even a copy of the report."

"Do you still have it?"

"Maybe. I've got some stuff from them. I'm not sure what."

"If you don't have the report, we'll need to get a copy. It could be important."

"Really? Why?"

"First let me see the paperwork. I'll know more then."

I wrote some notes on my legal pad and looked up. "Let's talk about those texts."

"I didn't do them, Rachel. I promise."

"But the stuff in those texts—those were very private family matters, Holly, like the time you supposedly caught your brother in your mother's bra and panties. That really happened, right?"

"It did." She turned to her sister. "Right?"

"Yep. A real pervert."

"And those texts—they certainly made your brother mad."

Holly nodded. "Absolutely. He was furious that day at the mediation, yelling at me about those texts. I had no idea what he was talking about. I swear."

"But someone else knew about those details, Holly—must have known they would get your brother upset."

"I suppose. But who?"

"Hah." Megan slapped her thigh and nodded. "Glasscock."

Holly turned to her. "Who?"

"Larry Glasscock." Megan turned to me with a grin. "Trust me, you don't forget a name like that."

"Who is he?" Holly asked.

"He contacted me about a year ago. He was looking for some old family photos."

"Of who?" I asked.

"Of all of us, and our parents—back when we were young. He found out that I'd inherited all of the family photo albums."

"Why did he want those photos?" I asked.

"He said he was doing a project for Alan."

"Did he say what kind?"

"He was vague. Sounded like maybe a biography or memoir or something like that."

"About your brother?" I said.

Megan nodded.

"And this Glasscock fellow. He was the one writing it?"

"I think so. Maybe. It wasn't all that clear to me."

"How did he contact you?"

"I think he just called. Introduced himself. Told me about the project. And asked if he could look at the photos."

"Did you let him?"

"I did. He seemed harmless enough."

"And?"

"He ended picking about a dozen photos. He had copies made."

"Larry Glasscock." I wrote the name down in my notes.

"Helluva name, eh?" Megan said.

"Was he from St. Louis?"

"I'm pretty sure he was."

"Did you ever hear from him after that?"

"Nope."

I leaned back in my chair. "Okay. This is a good start. Holly, see what paperwork you still have from those inspectors. Megan, if you have anything else on that Glasscock guy, let me know."

"Will do," Megan said.

"Meanwhile, I'll do some snooping around. We'll talk soon."

Chapter Twenty-One

The full name of the company was Bates Inspections LLC. Holly didn't have the report or any paperwork from the company, but it was easy to locate.

The Bates of Bates Inspections was J.R. Bates. I'd reached him on his cell phone Monday morning, explained my connection to Holly Goodman, and he agreed to meet me at his office in Kirkwood at three that afternoon.

J.R. Bates was a pleasant enough guy in his forties—lean and wiry with long dark hair combed straight back, a neatly trimmed goatee, and wire-rimmed glasses. He was in what I assume was his work outfit—tan work boots, faded jeans, and a blue chambray shirt with the sleeves rolled up above his elbows, revealing part of what appeared to be a U.S. Army tattoo on his right upper arm. He had that good-ol'-boy aura and a country Missouri accent, where the state's name is pronounced Missour-ah.

We were in his small, cluttered office, papers spread across his metal desk, a tool belt slung over a wooden sawhorse in the corner that seemed to function as a coatrack. He was leaning back in his chair, which was tilted against the wall. I was seated on the other side of the desk on a wobbly wooden chair.

"I did locate my files on that house, Miss Gold."

"Your client was MP Financial, right?"

"Actually, I technically had myself two clients. One after the other. Got to bill 'em both, too." He chuckled. "Nice work if you can get it."

"Who was the other client?"

"Mid-State Mortgage. I originally did the inspection for that MP Financial outfit, but them folks decided to pass on the deal. Apparently, Mrs. Goodman then applied for the refi with Mid-State. I'd done some work for those folks in the past and they give me a call when they received her application."

"Did you do a second inspection?"

"Naw. I told him I'd already done one and I'd let him see it for half price." He grinned and held his hands up, palms toward the ceiling. "Good deal for both of us."

"Mrs. Goodman said she recalls you giving her a copy of that report."

He nodded. "I most likely did. That's how I usually roll— one copy for the buyer or the bank, and an extra copy for the homeowner. I like to think of it as a good marketing practice. Most homeowners somewhere down the line end up being home buyers, and when that time come around, they'll need themselves an inspector."

"As I mentioned on the phone, Mrs. Goodman can't find her copy of the report."

"Well, I gotta tell you, Miss Gold, that report is closing in on one year, and that's bad news for her if she's planning to sell that house of hers and hoping to avoid another inspection. One year is getting to be your typical cutoff these days for lots of banks. Whoever is considering buying or refinancing that house is going to want a new inspection."

"She understands that, Mr. Bates. She doesn't have any present plan to sell or refinance. She just wants a copy for her records. She's willing to pay for it."

Bates waved his hand like he was swatting away a fly. "Ah, hell,

Miss Gold, I'm not gonna charge that nice lady. I made more than enough money on that report as it is. I'm happy to go grab you a copy for her. I must say she was an awfully nice gal. She ever get herself a new husband?"

"No."

"I'm a bit surprised. She was a mighty fine-looking woman. As are you, Miss Gold, if I do say so myself. Mighty fine. You tell her hi for me, would you now?"

———

"There they are," I said, pointing at the color photograph on page 11 of the inspection report that J.R. Bates had given me an hour ago.

Jacki Brand and I were standing side by side along my conference room table.

The photograph had been taken at an upward angle, aimed at what appeared to be a rusted water stain along the wall just below the basement ceiling. Visible below that water stain along the top shelf of a metal shelving unit were several different bottles and containers, including two red-capped white containers, each with a Henry Industries label that read "Potassium Cyanide—250 grams." Directly below those words was the red skull-and-crossbones poison symbol, and beneath that, in barely legible print size, was what appeared to be something about the product or its hazards.

Jacki leaned forward, arms behind her back, squinting. She nodded and straightened. "Yep."

I studied that photograph as I rubbed my chin.

Jacki said, "So that means someone inside Isaiah's company had access to that inspection report, and thus, access to that photo."

"Someone, yes. But technically MP Financial is a separate company."

"But a wholly owned subsidiary of the main company."

I nodded.

She flipped back to the first page and pointed. "That address?"

"Same as MP Enterprises. Different floor, same building."

Jacki looked at me. "So what do you know about this so far?"

"Beyond this," I gestured to the report, "just speculation."

"Such as?"

"Such as Holly was his sister, so I presume that whoever was handling the refinance paperwork would have notified Isaiah of the existence of that application and presumably, if asked, would have provided him with a copy of any other documents relevant to the application, including this report."

"What's the report say about that water stain?"

"I think he just flags it." I opened the report again to page eleven and leaned in close enough to read the text. "Yep He says the water stain appears to be from an old water leak from a pipe that must have been repaired. No evidence of recent leaking." I straightened. "So I'm assuming it wasn't the reason they declined the loan."

"Still," Jacki said, "whoever was reviewing the report for the loan application would have seen that photo and read the text beneath."

"True."

"Did that MP company give her a reason why they declined the loan?"

"No. Just a one-sentence rejection letter signed by one of the vice presidents. Her name was Janice, I think. I have a copy."

I flipped through my folder, removed a photocopy of that letter, and handed it to Jacki.

She studied it. "You're right. No reason given"

"I'm guessing the real reason was her brother's veto. They were already at odds with each other. She easily got the loan from a much bigger company."

"Janice Trotter," Jacki said. "Is she still there?"

"Good question."

"I'll call over there tomorrow. If she's still around, I'll see if she'll meet with me."

"Better yet," I said, "let's hope she's not still around and we can track her down. Might get more information if she's no longer on the payroll."

"True. Let's hope I have to track her down. What do you have on tomorrow?"

"I'm going to meet with that guy who was working on that memoir or whatever for Holly's brother. He's the one who made copies of some of the photos in Megan's family albums."

"You meeting him alone?"

"Actually, no. I'm having lunch with Benny over at Wash U, and then we're going to meet him together afterwards."

Jacki smiled. "Benny?"

I nodded. "Benny."

Jacki laughed. "Good Lord, Rachel, have you told Benny the guy's last name?"

"Not yet."

"Brace yourself, girl."

"I know." I sighed. "I will."

Chapter Twenty-Two

Larry Glasscock started his career in journalism nearly forty years ago as a reporter for the *St. Louis Post-Dispatch*, initially on the crime beat, later in features. He moved on to one of the regional papers as an editor of their features section, and when that paper folded about ten years ago he started his own business, Stories Worth Telling, LLC. According to his website, he offers consulting, editing, and writing services, primarily to aspiring writers and to those seeking someone to ghostwrite their personal story. On the drive over, I'd filled Benny in, including our pretext for the meeting, but waited until I'd parked in front of the apartment building before disclosing his name.

Benny's eyes widened. "Are you shitting me?"

I sighed. "No, Benny. That's his actual last name."

"That poor bastard."

"It's actually not even unusual. I checked the phone book. There are dozens of Glasscocks in St. Louis."

Benny started laughing again. "Still, can you imagine growing up with that last name? Or even worse, trying to get lucky in a singles bar and having to tell her your name?"

"Enough." I checked my watch. "He's probably in there waiting for us. And no jokes when we meet him."

Still grinning, Benny raised his right hand. "Scout's honor."

"Were you ever even a Boy Scout?"

"Actually, no. But on the subject of that poor bastard's last name, may I offer a brief medical lesson before we go."

"Oh, really, Doctor?"

"I'll keep it short. Medical science has confirmed that within the brain of every grown man, no matter how old or mature, lurks his seventh-grade avatar."

"And what exactly is this seventh-grade avatar?"

"The one who can't keep a straight face when he finds out this town's nickname is Mound City—or better yet, that there is actually a store in this town called Mound City Nuts."

"That name comes from the Indian Mounds across the river."

"You're missing the point, woman. We're talking seventh-grade boys. The same ones who believe that the three funniest people on the planet are the Three Stooges."

"Really? The Three Stooges?"

"Such a pity. You women are missing out on some mighty fine humor."

"I'll manage somehow. Now let's go see Mr.—uh, Larry."

He opened the passenger door. "Lead the way, gorgeous."

———

Larry Glasscock buzzed us up. His apartment was one of four on the second floor of the building. He opened the door halfway as we approached, his eyes flicking between Benny and me.

"Miss Gold?"

I smiled. "That's me. And this is my colleague, Professor Goldberg."

He gave me a nervous nod and opened the door wider. "Please come in."

We followed him into his apartment. He was a skinny little man—shorter than me, slightly hunched over. Bald on top, gray on the sides, big ears, wire-rimmed glasses, and a thick gray walrus mustache that covered his mouth. Somewhere in his late fifties or early sixties. White shirt, black sweater vest, baggy gray dress slacks, white tennis shoes.

He turned to us in his small living room and gestured toward the brown-and-yellow plaid couch. "Please have a seat."

As we did, he pulled up a chair facing us from the other side of the coffee table.

Once he was seated, I said, "Thank you for meeting with us, Mr. Glasscock."

He frowned. "I agreed to meet with you, Miss Gold, but I don't understand the purpose of the meeting."

"Let me explain. With the recent death of Mr. Blumenthal—"

"You mean the gentleman formerly known as Alan Blumenthal."

I smiled. "Same one. I represent his sister Megan Garber. As you recall, about one year ago, at your request, Ms. Garber allowed you to review her family photograph albums. You selected several photographs from those albums and Ms. Garber allowed you to make copies of them, correct?"

He rubbed his chin and nodded. "Eleven photographs in total."

"You informed Ms. Garber that you were working on a writing project for her brother—some sort of personal memoir—and that he might want to include one or more of those photographs in that publication. That's what you told her. Correct?"

He tugged on his right ear. After a moment, he said, "Yes."

"Did you ever complete that writing project for her brother?"

He continued to tug on his ear, frowning.

"Did you?"

"I'm not sure I can talk about that?"

"Why not?"

"The agreement they had me sign—the one for the writing project—there was this confidentiality clause. I couldn't tell anyone about the project."

Benny leaned forward. "The man is dead. You can probably talk if you avoid specifics."

Glasscock turned to Benny. "Really?"

"He's six feet under." Benny shrugged. "What can he do to you from down there?"

I said nothing and avoided eye contact with Benny as I tried to rationalize his sales pitch.

Glasscock thought it over. "Okay. Maybe I can talk about the project in general without going into the details. I don't want to get in any trouble. Anyway, I was finishing up the second draft when he died. He never got to see it."

"But he saw the first draft?" I asked.

Glasscock nodded. "I sent him the first draft, oh, about six months before he died."

"How did you send it?" I asked.

"By email."

"To him?"

He frowned. "I'd have to check. Either to him or maybe his secretary. A woman named Haddock, I think. Anyway, he definitely read that draft. We met to talk about the changes he wanted me to make."

"What kind of changes?" I asked.

"Mostly minor stuff in the first half. But he wanted me to really expand the second half."

"What exactly was this project? A memoir?"

"Yes and no." He paused, tugging on his ear. "When we first met, which was almost two years ago, Isaiah—that's what he insisted I call him—Isaiah gave me a copy of a book I'd never read before: *The Confessions of Saint Augustine*. Are you familiar with it?"

"Vaguely," I said. "We had to read parts of it in one of my college classes. It's the autobiography of the man who became Saint Augustine. He writes about his wicked early days, all the bad things he did as a young man, and then his eventual conversion to Christianity."

Glasscock nodded, eyes wide. "Exactly. Isaiah told me he saw parallels to his own life, and that's how he wanted me to structure the book."

"Saint Augustine?" I turned to Benny. "A role model for Isaiah?"

Benny shrugged. "That is one strange Orthodox Jew."

"Actually," Glasscock said, "we discussed that very issue after I read the book. Frankly, I had the same reaction at first—here was a Jewish man wearing one of those Jewish skullcaps whose role model was a Catholic saint? But it soon became clear to me that his admiration for Saint Augustine had nothing to do with religion and everything to do with personal transformation."

"So you were the ghost writer," I said, "How did you get the details of his life?"

"The usual way." He gestured toward his bookcase. "I've ghosted memoirs for other men, too. You get some of the details from boxes of old documents, such as high school yearbooks and letters home from overnight camp and teacher comments on grade school report cards and the like. But most of the substance comes from hours and hours of interviews with the subject."

"You did that with Isaiah?"

"I did. We met several times, and each interview lasted more than an hour."

"Where did you conduct the interviews?"

"All in his office."

"Did you take notes?"

"I did, but mostly in outline form. I recorded each session, and those are what I mainly relied on."

"Do you still have those tapes?"

He shook his head. "For other memoirs, yes. But not with Isaiah. He insisted that I give them all to him after I finished that first draft."

"Why?"

Glasscock shrugged. "It was in that agreement I signed."

"Did you keep a copy of those tapes?"

"No. I did not. That condition was in the agreement. He made sure I complied. He had his assistant come here and pick them up."

"Was that Miss Haddock?"

He shook his head. "It was a man."

"Do you remember his name?"

He grimaced, trying to remember. "No. A little guy."

"With a mustache?"

He smiled. "Yep. A little guy with a mustache."

"Has anyone at MP Enterprises contacted you since Isaiah's death?"

"No."

"Other than Isaiah and his secretary and that little guy with the mustache, did you have contact with anyone else in his organization?"

"I spoke with his, uh, I guess you'd say his significant other?"

"Anna?"

"Yes."

"For the memoir?"

"Yes. I interviewed her."

"Once?"

"Once."

"What did you talk about in the interview?"

He frowned and turned to Benny. "She's still alive, Professor. I'd need to check with her before I talk about that."

"Don't bother," I said. "I was just curious. No need to contact her."

"Okay." He looked relieved.

I looked down at my notes as I thought about how to phrase my next questions.

I turned to him. "Mr. Glasscock, I don't want to violate any confidentiality obligation of yours, so I'm going to keep my questions very general, okay?"

He gave me a puzzled look. "I suppose."

"This was a memoir or autobiography that Isaiah wanted you

to model on the structure and content of the Saint Augustine book, correct?"

"Yes."

"The Saint Augustine book describes some very personal actions and events of his youth, correct?"

"Yes."

"Including some actions that Saint Augustine viewed as immoral or embarrassing, correct?"

"Yes."

"And did you attempt to model the structure and content of Isaiah's memoir after the structure and content of the Saint Augustine book?"

He moved his head from side to side as he pondered the question. "To a certain extent, yes. Obviously, Saint Augustine's life was quite different from Isaiah's, and thus there were not many parallels."

"But your draft included some very personal events, including actions and events from Isaiah's youth, correct?"

"That's true. He didn't want me to whitewash anything from those days."

"Let me give you an example. One of his sisters told me about an incident that occurred back when she was a young girl. She said that she walked into her brother's bedroom without knocking and discovered him wearing nothing but his mother's bra and panties."

I paused.

Glasscock leaned back in his chair, glancing over at Benny and then back at me.

"My question to you, sir, is as follows: Is today the first time you ever heard about that incident?"

He tugged on his ear again.

I stared at him.

"Well?" I said.

"No. This was not the first time I heard about that incident."

Chapter Twenty-Three

We drove in silence back to the law school. I considered what Larry Glasscock had confirmed while Benny scrolled through emails on his cell phone.

I pulled into the parking lot and stopped next to Benny's car.

"Thanks," I said.

Benny looked up from his phone with a frown and shook his head.

"What?" I asked.

"Not enough."

"What's not enough?"

"That putz put those family secrets into a manuscript that gets read by Isaiah, but unless you think Little Larry Glass Dick is the killer, you need to get those secrets into some other hands, especially inside that company."

"Agreed, and preferably not through a subpoena in the criminal case. Assuming Holly is innocent, I don't want to tip my hand to the prosecutor."

"But you still need a court order, right? You'll never get that information from the company without a court order."

"You're probably right."

"But what other courtroom option do you have?"

I smiled. "God bless you, Benny. You are a genius."

"True—and maybe, at long last, a finalist for *People* magazine's Sexiest Antitrust Professor. But I confess that I'm not following you here."

"I *do* have another courtroom option,"

"Oh?"

"Yep. And at the risk of tapping into your seventh-grade brain, that option is the one and only Silvio Maccarone."

Benny frowned. "Huh?"

"Let me explain."

———

And the following afternoon I was back before the Honorable Silvio Maccarone on my emergency motion for a protective order seeking all documents in the custody or control of MP Enterprises that in any way related to Larry Glasscock and the scope of his employment, including all drafts, documents, and communications.

I'd been able to file that motion before Judge Maccarone because I did so on behalf of Megan Garber, in her personal capacity, as the heir and guardian of the rights of publicity of her deceased mother and father, and, most important for that motion, as successor trustee of the Peggy R. Blumenthal Trust. Although I also included Holly in the motion, the connection to the Peggy R. Blumenthal Trust insured we'd be back before Judge Maccarone.

And once again, MP Enterprises was represented by Yale Rockwell and his pack of lawyers, and once again the client's seat at counsel table was occupied by Anna. Seated directly behind Anna in the first row of the galley were Arthur Bell, who was busy texting on his cell phone when we arrived, and Isaiah's secretary, Mildred Haddock, who glared at me as I passed her on my way to counsel's table. I was surprised to see the two of them in court, but perhaps Rockwell requested their presence in case he needed to put one or both on the witness stand.

Judge Maccarone frowned down at me. "Now who exactly is this G-g-g-glasscock gentleman, Counsel?"

"He's a freelance writer, Your Honor. We understand that he was hired by either MP Enterprises or by its late CEO."

"For what purpose?"

"Again, we have not seen the agreement with Mr. Glasscock, but we understand that he was hired to write the autobiography of the late CEO."

"When you say the late CEO, you mean Mr. Blumenthal, correct?" Judge Maccarone turned toward Yale Rockwell and shook his head. "That is, the Blumenthal who decided for some l-l-loony reason to start calling himself Isaiah."

I glanced over and saw Anna flinch in anger.

Judge Maccarone continued. "That's the CEO guy, right?"

I turned back to the judge and nodded. "Yes, Your Honor."

"So what exactly is your p-p-p-problem, counsel?"

"In the course of his writing duties," I said, "Mr. Glasscock asked for and was given permission to review family photograph albums in the possession of Ms. Garber."

I gestured toward Megan, who was seated with Holly at my counsel's table.

"Mr. Glasscock made copies of eleven highly personal photographs that included images of Ms. Garber, her sister, and her parents. We don't know the status of that manuscript. We don't know what personal details, true or false, are included in those pages. And we don't know the role, if any, to be played by those photographs in the publication. It is our further understanding, based on a conversation with Mr. Glasscock, that he is bound by a strict confidentiality agreement and that the rest of the project is veiled in secrecy. We come before the Court today merely to ask to lift that veil."

"Outrageous," Yale Rockwell announced, getting to his feet. He pointed his index finger at me. "This woman seeks a prior restraint, Your Honor. Unbelievable. A prior restraint in violation of our most sacred and hallowed right of freedom of speech, as protected by the First Amendment to the United States Constitution. It reminds me of that saying by—"

"Enough!" Judge Maccarone shouted, pointing his gavel at Rockwell. "Sit down!"

Rockwell, his face contorted in anger, sat down.

The judge turned to me with a puzzled look. "A p-p-prior restraint?"

"No, Your Honor. As I said, we merely ask the Court to allow us to lift that veil—to allow what is commonly known in the publishing industry as a pre-publication review. Ms. Garber and Ms. Goodman have privacy rights, and they have the right to protect their reputations. And Ms. Garber, as the heir of the rights of publicity of her beloved parents, has a legal and a moral obligation to protect their rights as well. If our review of the relevant material reveals no issues of concern, you will not hear from us again. But if we do come across a passage that would violate one of my clients' rights or falsely damage one of their reputations, we merely would request the opportunity to return to this court, in accordance with due process, to seek appropriate relief if we are unable to convince Mr. Blumenthal's representatives to revise that passage. So we do not seek a prior restraint, Your Honor."

"No? Then what do you seek?"

"We merely ask the Court for patience and for an opportunity, if it should come to pass, to try to avoid a lawsuit for invasion of privacy or defamation. Or"—and here I turned toward Yale Rockwell and gave him my most insincere smile—"if Mr. Rockwell would prefer to phrase it, provide him a rare opportunity to sacrifice a large and lucrative legal fee in order to help his client avoid an expensive and distracting lawsuit."

Which, as I hoped, relit his fuse.

"Avoid a lawsuit?" he snarled, rising to his feet, his face beet red. "Bring it on, lady. Bring it on."

Bang!

Judge Maccarone clenched the gavel in his fist, having raised it again to shoulder height, his arm shaking.

"I've heard enough, especially f-f-f-from you, Mr. Rockwell. I will grant this motion."

He pointed the gavel at Rockwell. "Your client—or clients—have three days to turn over every single d-d-d-document regarding whatever work this Glasscock fellow was doing, including any agreement with him, any drafts, any email communications. Whatever. Turn it over or f-f-f-face sanctions."

He turned to me. "Draft the order, counsel."

"I will. Thank you, Your Honor."

He turned to glare at Yale Rockwell, who was staring down at his legal pad, flushed and shaking his head.

The judge banged the gavel hard and called, "Next case!"

Chapter Twenty-Four

Jacki read the court order and looked up with a smile. "Three days, eh?"

I nodded. "Yep. Three days."

Jacki reached across my desk for a fist bump. "Nice going, girlfriend."

We bumped.

I'd just filled Jacki in on the events from earlier that afternoon before the Honorable Silvio Maccarone.

I leaned back in my chair. "I'm afraid I'm not going to get a holiday card this year from Yale Rockwell."

"I think he's already given you a gift this year."

"Let's hope so. We'll see when we open that gift in three days. We still have some big gaps to fill in."

"Speaking of which," Jacki said with a smile.

"Really?" I leaned forward. "You found her?"

"I did."

"Janice, right?"

"Full name: Janice Ellen Trotter. She left MP Financial about three months ago."

"And now?"

"A loan officer at US Bank. Works out of one of their West County offices."

"So you guys talked?"

"We did. She was nervous at first. I promised her the conversation would be off the record. I assured her that it would be a lot easier and lot faster than the alternative, which was getting served with a subpoena and testifying under oath. She agreed. We met for coffee at a nearby Starbucks."

"Fill me in."

"Okay." Jacki opened her notebook and scanned her notes. "So Janice worked at MP Financial for a little over four years. The original company was Mound City Mortgage. That's who hired her. About a year later, MP Enterprises acquired the company and changed its name. The management remained pretty much the same after the acquisition. Other than the annual holiday party in December and the annual family picnic event in the summer, there was little interaction with the parent company."

"Did she ever have any direct dealings with Isaiah?"

Jacki shook her head. "He visited their offices once or twice each year, but always for meetings limited to the management team. She would see him in the conference room on those visits but never spoke with him."

"Does she remember anything about Holly's application to refinance her home mortgage?"

Jacki raised her eyebrows. "That's where it gets interesting."

"Let's hear it."

"The application ended up on Janice's desk. Her supervisor"—she paused to look at her notes—"Brian Fedder, told her that Holly was Isaiah's sister. Janice told me that made her extra diligent. Although she assumed that the loan approval was pretty much foreordained, she also assumed that her work product might be reviewed by people way higher up. So she made sure she crossed every 't' and dotted every 'i' before she prepared her memo approving the loan. She told me she was proud of her work product when she gave the file to her boss."

"What did the file include?"

"There was her memo and all the usual paperwork attached— credit report, inspection report, and so on. Normally, she said, he would be the one to make the final decision, but he told her he was under orders to send it upstairs. Which was all fine with her. Better than fine, actually, since she was proud of her work and eager to have the higher-ups see it."

"And then?"

Jacki raised her eyebrows and shook her head. "And then her approval memo came back from upstairs two days later with a big APPLICATION REJECTED on the first page."

"Did they give any reasons?"

"None. She was surprised and confused. There had been rejections in the past, but always with an explanation. Not this time."

"Did she try to find out why?"

"She asked her boss. He said he didn't know. No one told him, either. And he actually tried to find out. He called upstairs—or at least that's what he told her."

"Did he tell her who he talked to?"

"She doesn't recall. She said he told her he was never given the reason. Just that the application was rejected."

"Did she have any contact with anyone up on the top floor?"

"Yeah. She thinks her contact was his secretary."

"Does she remember the name?"

"No, but she said the woman sounded old and was definitely grumpy."

"Sounds like Mildred Haddock, aka Frau Farbissina."

"That was Isaiah's secretary, right?"

"That's her. You said Janice's approval memo came back with that rejection notice. Did all the other paperwork come back as well?"

"I asked her. She said no. Just the memo."

I leaned back in my chair and smiled. "Interesting."

"My thought exactly."

"Anything else?"

Jacki scanned her notes. "I asked her about others at the company, about their general attitude about dealing with Isaiah and the rest of the parent company. She said there was a lot of grumbling. In fact, that's one of the reasons she jumped at the offer from US Bank."

Jacki paused to slowly read a page of her notes.

She looked up. "Here's an interesting irony. No one was crazy about the parent company. The camaraderie from the Mound City days died after the acquisition. More rules, more restrictions. But the unhappiest employee was a guy named Alonzo Flynn."

"Flynn?" I frowned. "I've heard that name before."

"He was their IT guy. Computers, software, web-based services, and the like."

"What was the irony?"

"Alonzo used to rant and complain about MP Enterprises, and especially Isaiah and Anna. He couldn't stand the two of them."

"Why?"

"Janice didn't know the reason. She assumes he must have had some direct dealings with one or both of them. Anyway, the month before she left the company Flynn got transferred upstairs to MP Enterprises. Although her boss—that Fedder guy—tried to pitch it to the group as a promotion, Flynn was not happy. He'd been in charge of all IT for MP Financial, but now he would be reporting to the chief technology officer at the parent company, and he viewed the change as a demotion."

"Alonzo Flynn," I repeated. "Hates Isaiah. Angry because he thinks he's been demoted."

"Intriguing, eh?"

"I'm thinking we need to come up with a pretext to meet Mr. Flynn."

"I'm thinking we'll be able to come up with that pretext."

I reached across my desk for a fist bump. "Nice going, girlfriend."

We bumped.

Chapter Twenty-Five

I place the gray stone on top of Jonathan's headstone, next to the one that Sam and I had placed there last Sunday. I take a deep breath, lay my hand on the cool granite, and close my eyes.

These visits are my version of meditation even though there is plenty here to disrupt any serenity, beginning with the side-by-side headstones of Jonathan and his first wife Robyn. The pair of dates etched onto each headstone is stark evidence of life's profound injustice. And while I continue to light candles and say the blessings on Friday night and go to shul to say Kaddish on Jonathan's yahrzeit and on my father's yahrzeit, Jonathan's death—coupled with his first wife's death and the tragedies that have befallen some of my friends—has challenged my faith. What does it mean, I ask myself, to believe in a God who would allow such terrible things to happen to such good people?

My mother has long since resolved that question, having lost most of her family in the Holocaust. She remains a proud and defiant Jew, but her version of Judaism is purely cultural.

"An almighty God?" she says with a dismissive snort. "Trust me, Rachela, it's a *bubbe meise.*" Translation: a grandmother's fable.

At the foot of the two graves is a granite memorial bench with WOLF carved on the front. I take a seat there and try to get my thoughts and emotions under control. Over the past year or so I have learned to narrow my focus to Jonathan's grave and ignore the surroundings. That's because to the left of Robyn's headstone is a double headstone for her father (who had died two years before Robyn) and her mother (who is still alive), and to the left of those headstones is an entire row of tightly packed gravesites. To the right of Jonathan's headstone stands a large memorial for the Schwartz family, several of whom are buried in a row. The result, when I sit alone on the memorial bench, is an acute sense of solitude. There will be no room for anyone else.

I start, as always, with a silent update of his three children—my two stepdaughters and our son, Sam. There is good news to share about each one, and I do so with a deep sense of gratitude for my good fortune in having such wonderful children.

Then I take him through my step-by-step efforts to find a way into the executive suite of MP Enterprises, including what Jacki had learned today from Janice Trotter, the former loan officer at the MP subsidiary, and the IT guy named Alonzo Flynn.

And then it is on to Eli Contini's case.

"Did you know him?" I rear back, realizing I'd asked that question aloud. I glance around. No one is nearby.

I explain our frustration in trying to find a photograph of Cissy Robb at the Carousel Auction Gala at the Ritz-Carlton held that critical weekend. The *Post-Dispatch* photographer has none. Even more frustrating, we'd been able to contact the photographer from the *Ladue News* who covered the event. Although the print edition has no photograph of Cissy, we had hoped he might have one among his other photos of the event. Ironically, he did have one of her husband Robbie, posing with three other tuxedoed men, all hoisting wineglasses, but not one of Cissy.

But I save the best—or maybe the worst—or probably the weirdest—for last.

"Guess what else, Jonathan?" I say softly, pausing to make sure there is no one in earshot. "My mother says it's time already with me and Abe, and by 'time' you know what she's talking about. Oy, she is definitely one of a kind."

I smile and shake my head.

"He's a good man, Jonathan. He's not you. There'll never be another you. But you'd like him. I know you would. He's got a good heart."

I stand, walk over to his headstone, place my hand on top, lean down, and whisper, "I'll keep you posted, sweetie."

Chapter Twenty-Six

"Here we go," Jacki said.

She was seated in our workroom in front of the computer—the one with the two-foot-wide LED monitor, large enough for two people to work side by side.

I came around, sat next to her, and stared at the screen.

"The Weasel, eh?" I said.

"Yep."

"So this is the first document?"

"The first of what they produced to us."

This was the cache of documents—electronic and otherwise—that Judge Maccarone had ordered MP Enterprises to produce to us.

Displayed on the screen was an email from almost a year ago:

To: Larry Glasscock
From: Arnold Bell, Senior Aide to the Chairman
Re: The Autobiography Project

Attached is the Collaboration Agreement you discussed with the Chairman, along with the Nondisclosure Agreement. I can assure you that all involved in this project, including myself, are required to sign a nondisclosure agreement. Your retention shall commence promptly upon return of an executed copy of said Agreements. I need not emphasize that time is of the essence.

"Can you open the documents?" I said, pointing at the email attachments.

Jacki clicked on first attachment, which opened into the Collaboration Agreement between Isaiah and Larry Glasscock covering his writing of Isaiah's memoir. We read through it together, page by page. It was a fairly standard ghostwriter agreement, and thus clogged with legalese. Payment terms: $5,000 upon signing, and then five additional $5,000 payments at various stages in the process. As stated in the agreement, the sole credited author of the published version of the book was to be Isaiah. The second document—the Nondisclosure Agreement—went beyond the usual provision to create a relatively stiff financial penalty—$250,000—if Glasscock ever disclosed his role in the creation of the autobiography or any of the contents of the autobiography prior to publication.

"Interesting," I said. "So Arnold had to sign one, too."

"Which means he probably saw the drafts, presumably along with Anna and Isaiah's secretary Mildred."

The next email, two days later, was from Glasscock back to Arnold Bell attaching signed copies of the Collaboration Agreement and the Nondisclosure Agreement.

Nothing for nine days, and then:

To: Larry Glasscock
From: Mildred Haddock, Assistant to the Chairman
Re: The Autobiography Project

Please be advised that the Chairman will be available for the initial Project interview in his offices tomorrow at 1:15 p.m. Be prompt.

And thus it began. An email scheduling a Project interview. A week or two of silence. Then another scheduling email, and another period of email silence. The first four scheduling emails were from Mildred Haddock, with no one cc'ed or bcc'ed and apparently with no response from Glasscock required to confirm the appointment.

The next email communication was three weeks after that fourth interview:

To: Mildred Haddock
From: Larry Glasscock
Re: The Autobiography Project

Dear Ms. Haddock:

Per my discussion with the Chairman during our last meeting, I attach a draft of the proposed synopsis of his autobiography. Once he has had an opportunity to review it, we should schedule the next meeting to discuss it and related matters. Thank you.

Sincerely,
Larry

"Let's take a look," I said.

Jacki clicked on the attachment, which opened into a two-page Word document, the first of which was a cover page.

"Oh gimme a break," she groaned as we stared at that page:

SYNOPSIS OF
THE NEW BOOK OF ISAIAH:
THE INSPIRING STORY OF A VISIONARY
ENTREPRENEUR

I groaned. "Be still my heart. Okay, let's see the next page."

The synopsis was, thankfully, just two paragraphs:

This is the stirring account of the remarkable trans-formation of a seemingly ordinary young man named Alan Blumenthal into Isaiah ben Moishe, a legendary businessman and role model esteemed from Wall Street to Davos. How did this astonishing change take place? How did a boy often shamed by a stern and demanding father, a young man tormented by what he perceived as his own shortcomings, become a titan of industry—a powerhouse who eventually taught his own father the meaning of shame?

This is the story of an American Dream, a story that the nation has been waiting to hear—a story journalists have pursued in vain for years, thwarted repeatedly by Isaiah's unwillingness to allow any invasion of his sacred privacy. But that was then, back before he heard the calling from on high to tell his story, to inspire the young men and women of this country, to help them understand that greatness is within their grasp. Yes, this is the long-awaited *New Book of Isaiah*.

Jacki snorted. "Really, dude? The man is delusional."

"Was. Past tense."

"Still, this is outrageous. And disgusting." Jacki gestured at the screen and shook her head. "His story is the one that's supposed to inspire young men and women that greatness is within their grasp? Are you kidding me? This jerk was nothing more than a member of the lucky sperm club. The only thing within his grasp was the multimillion-dollar company his daddy created. All he did was steal it and screw over his daddy."

"Agreed. He was a creep." I gestured toward the screen. "But let's keep going."

Next came three more emails to Glasscock scheduling interviews with the Chairman, followed by a two-month communication gap, then an email from Glasscock to Haddock:

To: Mildred Haddock
From: Larry Glasscock
Re: The Autobiography Project

Dear Ms. Haddock:

Please let the Chairman know that I had the opportunity to review those family photo albums at the home of his sister Megan, who was quite hospitable. I found several good shots that should fit nicely within the book's themes and events. Thank you.

Sincerely,
Larry

Another two-month gap, and then the following:

To: Mildred Haddock
From: Larry Glasscock
Re: The Autobiography Project

Dear Ms. Haddock:

I have attached for the Chairman's review a rough first draft of his autobiography. I emphasize that this is just a first draft. I will be pleased to meet him at this convenience after he has had an opportunity to review my work.

Also, please advise Mr. Bell that this submission constitutes the trigger for the second payment under the Collaboration Agreement.

Thank you.
Sincerely,
Larry

"Finally," I said.

Jacki clicked on the attachment, and it opened into a 276-page word document titled *The New Book of Isaiah*.

After the title page came a page titled Section 1 with the following quote beneath it:

> *"I will now call to mind my past foulness, and the*
> *carnal corruptions of my soul; not because I love*
> *them, but that I may love Thee, O my God."*
> —*The Confessions of Saint Augustine*

"We can read this manuscript later," I said. "Let's see if we can source those three texts."

Jacki turned to me. "What texts?"

"The ones Holly allegedly sent to her brother." I pointed at the screen. "Do a search for panties."

"Really?"

"Really."

Jack clicked the Find icon, typed in "panties," and hit Return.

The following appeared in the Search Results frame:

1 result

> Page 43: "…the house. Standing naked before the full-length mirror on my bedroom door, I slipped on the **panties**, and then, with some difficulty, put on the bra. As I stared at my reflection, the door suddenly swung open and…"

"Open that page, Jacki."

She did.

While the full description of the panties-and-bra incident apparently started before page 43 and continued after page 43, there were enough details on that page to get the gist of the story, namely, a conflicted boy on the cusp of puberty sneaks into his parents' bedroom one Saturday afternoon, removes a pair of panties and a bra from his mother's dresser, and—in the belief that he is the only one in the house—strips naked and puts them on, only to have his younger sister barge into his room at that exact moment, catching him not only in the act of striking a sexy pose in the mirror but a pose made even more striking by an erection.

"I hate to say it," Jacki said, "but I can relate. Did the same thing at his age—more than once, in fact—but was never caught."

"And, thank goodness, never became a self-proclaimed prophet." I checked my notes. "Try a search for firecracker."

And we turned up, on page 57, the tale of the twenty-dollar bill he stole from his father's wallet to buy firecrackers.

Our search for *"bat mitzvah"* resulted in eleven hits, the seventh of which—beginning on page 87—described his drunken escapades at his sister Megan's *bat mitzvah* party that culminated in a power barf splattering the dance floor and horrifying the guests doing the Macarena.

Jacki chuckled. "That must have been a sight."

"Wow," I said, "he was one troubled young man."

"And one creepy one, too. You want me to print the manuscript now?"

"It can wait. Let's see what else they included in their production."

"There's not much. Just a few more emails."

"Keep your fingers crossed," I said.

"For what?"

"We have the manuscript, and we've confirmed that it

contains all the necessary personal details for those three texts. And we've confirmed that manuscript reached the executive floor."

"And was received by his secretary from Glasscock."

"Yep, and presumably it was printed off for Isaiah to read. But it would be nice to confirm that someone up there actually read it beside Isaiah. Just because she printed off for him doesn't mean she read it."

Jacki nodded. "Okay."

There was a seventeen-day lag between the email with the manuscript and the next one, which was just a one-sentence email from Mildred Haddock to Larry Glasscock scheduling a telephone conference with Isaiah for the following afternoon. That was followed two days later by another email from Haddock to Glasscock scheduling a telephone conference. Four days later, Glasscock sent to Haddock an email with an attachment that he described as "a revised manuscript incorporating the Chairman's comments and edits."

Jacki opened that version of the manuscript, and we confirmed that the three key incidents from the first draft all remained in that draft. The only difference between the two manuscripts that we could detect without a full-scale comparison was an expanded chapter on the various business successes under Isaiah's leadership.

Six days later, another email from Haddock to Glasscock scheduling a telephone conference.

Twelve days of silence, and then:

To: Arnold Bell
Cc: Isaiah, A. Flynn
From: Anna
Re: The Autobiography Project—Fact-Check

We have reached the fact-check stage of the above-referenced Project, and as you will see, the manuscript has been reformatted in a more readable publishing template. I am having Ms. Haddock deliver to your office a copy of the manuscript with every factual assertion needing confirmation highlighted in yellow. As you will see, all the highlighted statements related to transactions and other events concerning MP Enterprises. You must confirm the accuracy of each such statement. Some of that confirmation information will be available in minutes of the board meetings. Others in the relevant transaction files. Isaiah emphasizes the importance of insuring the accuracy of all statements regarding activities of MP Enterprises. He reminds you that this must be treated as a high-priority item. Just as important, you must maintain the highest level of confidentiality regarding all matters involving this Project. Thus you cannot delegate these important tasks to someone else in the company.

"Well, well, well," I said. "Look who must have done the reformatting of that manuscript. Mr. Flynn. We have our pretext, Jacki."

Nine days later, Arnold Bell sent Anna a two-sentence email:

Placed manuscript on your chair this morning. As you will see, each highlighted portion has either been confirmed as accurate (and thus marked with a check) or corrected in red pen.

Two days later, Mildred Haddock sent an email to Glasscock—the last email in the production—showing cc's to Anna, Bell, and Flynn:

The manuscript has been reviewed for accuracy by Mr. Bell and Anna. Attached are scanned copies of the corrected pages. These corrections have been made on the electronic copy in the Chairman's possession. You are instructed to make the corrections on your copy as well.

I leaned back in my chair. "Mission accomplished."

"So all three of them saw the contents of that manuscript."

"Actually, all four of them. If Alonzo Flynn did the formatting, we have a perfectly legitimate reason to talk to him. Remember, this all started with our request to review the manner in which those family photographs were going to be used in the memoir. If Flynn did the formatting, then he should know the answer to that issue."

"So what's next?"

I turned to Jacki and smiled. "Time to call the president of the Judge Maccarone Fan Club."

"That would be the charming Yale Rockwell?"

"Yep."

Chapter Twenty-Seven

The meeting with Alonzo Flynn was easy to set up—probably because Yale Rockwell couldn't stomach the prospect of another hearing before Judge Maccarone. I had pitched the meeting to him as a simple follow-up, explaining that the emails they had provided to us per the Judge's order indicated that Flynn was the employee responsible for formatting Isaiah's memoir, and thus the person most knowledgeable as to the placement and context of those family photographs.

I assumed that Rockwell would nevertheless send one of his firm's young lawyers to the meeting, and thus Jacki came along for the sole purpose of distracting that lawyer—a role I knew she would play well. Jacki's target that day turned out to be an obviously nervous twenty-something guy name Marvin in an ill-fitting gray suit and red bow tie. Jacki was in fine form. Between the time Marvin met us at the elevator on the eleventh floor of the MP Enterprises building and when we reached Alonzo Flynn's tiny windowless office somewhere in the interior of that floor, Marvin and Jacki were deeply immersed in a spirited discussion about some recent rounds of five-card stud on a cable TV show called something like *Poker in America*. Turns out Marvin was a big fan, and Jacki, dating back to her

Granite City steelworker days, had been somewhat of a legend at the casino poker tables.

And thus they were out of earshot in the hall when I stepped into the little office where a fat man in his thirties, seated with his back to the door, was squinting at his computer screen.

"Mr. Flynn?"

He turned toward me with a frown.

"I'm Rachel Gold."

He nodded, still frowning.

The first things you notice about Alonzo Flynn—or at least the first things I noticed—were the arm tattoos: elaborate black-and-scarlet filigrees that started at his wrists, continued up his pudgy arms through the short sleeves of his blue plaid shirt and crested under his chin. Then came the brass nose ring and the shaggy red curly hair and the acne scars and the thick horn-rimmed glasses. The plaid shirt, unbuttoned at the neck, was stretched tight across his big belly, and his faded olive-green cargo pants were slightly frayed at the bottoms of both legs..

I sat down in the guest chair and gave him a friendly smile. "Thank you for meeting with me. I just have a few questions for you."

"This is about that book?"

"Yes. Isaiah's memoir. I understand you were in charge of formatting it for publication."

"So what?"

"We were given a copy of the last draft. In putting together the book, Mr. Glasscock collected eleven family photographs from one of Isaiah's sisters."

"Which sister?" Flynn was grinning. "The one who caught him in his mommy's bra and panties?"

"So you read the manuscript?"

He shrugged. "Here and there. Glasscock couldn't format his way out of paper bag. There was a lot of reformatting to do."

"We couldn't tell from our copy of the document which of

those photographs were going to be included in the book and in what context."

"Can't help you there, lady."

"Why not?"

"As far as I know, the big guy died before they decided which ones to use and where to put them. I had them all scanned and ready to insert, but I never got any instructions."

"Who'd you ask?"

He paused, tugging at his right ear. "Maybe that Glasscock guy. Or maybe Miss Haddock."

"What about Isaiah?"

"What about him?"

"Did you ask him?"

He snorted. "Ask Isaiah? No fucking way, lady."

"Why not?"

"Isaiah? He wouldn't talk to someone like me."

"How do you know that?"

"I know it. First off, you couldn't get in there unless you made an appointment with that nasty secretary."

"Miss Haddock?"

"Yep. And your chances of her giving you an appointment were slim to none. I'm down here on the eleventh floor, and he never came down here. Ever. And even if he did, the rules were you couldn't approach him on your own."

"Were you ever up on that floor?"

"Of course. Probably several times a week. I'm in IT. Whenever one of them up there has a computer issue—or when we have to update their software—I'm up there. It isn't like you need a hall pass or any bullshit like that."

"Unless you wanted to see Isaiah."

He snorted. "Exactly."

"I sense you weren't a big fan of his."

He leaned back in his chair and stared at me. "Why do you say that?"

"Just the way you talk about him."

"Hey, he was the boss and we were the underlings." He gave me a shrug that looked more forced than nonchalant. "Believe me, I wasn't the only one. Big guy didn't have many fans in this company."

"What about Anna?" I asked.

A pause. "What about her?"

"In your work on the book did you have any dealings with her?"

"You mean direct dealings?" He laughed. "No way. That bitch wouldn't stoop to my level. Other than an occasional email, no contact at all."

"What about if she had a computer problem?"

"The rule was you didn't enter her office unless she was gone. And even then you could only go in if you were accompanied by her assistant. That Anna—she's a real piece of work."

There was a beep on his computer. He turned toward the screen, squinted at something, and turned back to me. "Got a computer glitch down in accounting. Ninth floor." He stood. "We all done here?"

"For now. I may have some follow-up questions."

"Fair enough."

"One last question, Alonzo."

"Call me Al. Everyone else does."

"Okay, Al. Do you know that status of Isaiah's memoir?"

"Status?"

"Is it going to be published?"

"Good question." He scratched his neck. "Seemed like just a silly vanity project before. But now that's he been murdered, hell, might be some real sales potential there, eh? Not that it matters to me, though."

"Why not?"

He rubbed his thumb against his fingers in a money gesture. "No Benjamins in it for me, even if it is a bestseller. Then again, no Benjamins in it for Isaiah, either." He chuckled. "Not when you're six feet under."

———

I filled Jacki in on our way back to the office.

"Wow. He certainly wasn't afraid to tell you his feelings about Isaiah."

"He despised him, Jacki. That is for sure."

"But the way he talked about him—not exactly the way you'd expect a killer to talk."

"How so?"

"If he were guilty, you'd think he'd try to hide his feelings about his victim. Maybe show a little sympathy."

"That's possible. But if he was the one who set the whole thing up, he might believe that Holly's conviction is a sure thing, which would mean he was free to talk trash about the dead man. He's definitely a cocky guy. And arrogant enough to believe he's invulnerable."

"I suppose so."

"Oh, well." I shook my head. "I was hoping we'd be able to cross him off our list after I had a chance to meet with him."

"Not yet."

"Agreed."

Chapter Twenty-Eight

It was a lovely Sunday afternoon in the park, warm and sunny and slightly breezy—a perfect autumn day for soccer. Sam's team was tied one-to-one at halftime. He and his first-grade teammates were seated on the grass in a semicircle facing their coach, listening to her comments and instructions as they nibbled on orange slices.

It should have been a perfect autumn day for me as well, a day to disconnect from my legal practice and relax and appreciate my surroundings, but instead I stood along the sidelines, head down, reading through my emails, which only seemed to multiply over the weekends.

"Good afternoon, Rachel Gold."

I turned.

The speaker was a heavyset man in his early forties with a prominent nose, dark slicked-back hair, and aviator sunglasses. He wore a snug gray t-shirt that bulged at his belly, black jeans, and tan boat shoes with no socks. And a fancy silver Rolex watch. And a wedding ring.

He smiled. "Good to see you again."

I gazed at him. "Do we know each other?"

He chuckled. "Probably not. I was up in the stands that day."

"What day was that?"

"The big football game: Ladue versus U. City."

"When?"

"Back in high school. I was a senior at Ladue. You would have been, oh, a sophomore, probably. Like I say, I was up in the stands. You were out there on the field. Well, mostly on the sidelines. You were our favorite U. City cheerleader that day. My buddies all agreed: hottest gal on the squad. Not even close."

He oozed a smarmy aura.

I forced a smile. "But we never met."

"Correcto." He chuckled again. "My bad."

"And your name is?"

"Good question." Another chuckle. "Back then it was Rubenstein. Richie Rubenstein."

"And now?"

"Shortened it after college. Better for business. Which is the reason I'm here today."

"Shortened it to what?"

"Robb. Richie Robb."

I frowned. It seemed vaguely familiar.

"You've met my wife," he said. "Cissy Robb."

I stared at him, and then noticed a tall, muscle-bound man in sweat pants and a tight black t-shirt standing about ten yards behind Robb, staring at us, arms akimbo, head shaved, wraparound sunglasses.

I turned back to Robb, "Why are you here?"

He smiled. "I'm on a mission of peace. Here to encourage you and your client to settle the lawsuit."

"It doesn't work that way, Mr. Robb."

"Call me Richie."

"Actually, Mr. Robb, if you don't leave, I'll call your wife's lawyer."

"He'll be fine. No biggie. We're strictly off the record here, Rachel. Just the two of us, trying to find a way for you and your client to extricate yourself from this clusterfuck of a lawsuit before you both get humiliated in court."

"We're done here. Time for you and your guardian to leave."

"Don't be foolish. Hey, maybe my wife got a little carried away that day. Shit happens, right? Believe me, it fucking happens. But in the long run who gives a rat's ass about that dress? Three years from now it'll be just another schmatta to drop off at Goodwill. But now, well, I can make this all go away pain-free. Maybe even sweeten the deal with a little incentive for you and your client. All confidential of course."

"I said we're done. Get out of here."

He took a step closer, his anger visible. "Listen to me, bitch. Never underestimate Richie Robb. I can make this end happily for you—or I can make this end unhappily for you. Very unhappily. I guarantee it."

"Is that a threat, Mr. Robb?"

"You better believe it. You just got threatened, bitch. Big-time. Guaranteed."

"Good. Because guess what? I can make this end unhappily for you, too. Very unhappily. I guarantee it."

He frowned. "What the fuck are talking about?"

I held up my iPhone. "This is what I'm talking about, Little Richie. I've recorded our entire conversation."

I gestured toward the parking lot.

"See that police car? Unless you want to call your attorney and arrange for bail, you and your tough guy better get out of here now."

"She's right."

I turned. One of the other moms—Billy's mother—had stepped at my side.

"I'm her witness," she said. "I heard everything you said."

Robb looked at her and then at me and then toward the police car and then back to me and then turned toward that big guy.

"We're outta here," he said to the big guy, who dropped his arms and nodded.

Robb turned back to me, his face bright red. "Fuck you, Rachel Gold."

He turned to Billy's mom. "And you, too."

We watched the two of them stomp off toward the parking lot. They got into a black Cadillac Escalade SUV—the big guy behind the wheel. Robb gave me the finger as he climbed into the vehicle on the passenger side. The engine revved loudly three times, and then the SUV pulled out of the park.

I turned to Billy's mom. "Thanks, Cheryl."

She shook her head in disgust. "What a jerk."

I shrugged. "Pretty much what I expected."

"I can't believe you taped him. I'm impressed."

"Don't be," I said. "That was a bluff."

"No!" Her eyes widened. "Really?"

I winked and pressed my index finger against my lips. "Our secret."

She nodded and made a zipping gesture over her closed her lips.

I turned toward the field.

"Rachel," she said.

I looked back.

She had a big smile. "I didn't know you were a cheerleader, Rachel."

"Oy." I shook my head. "Later. The second half started."

Chapter Twenty-Nine

"It has to be one of those four."

"I agree," Jacki said. "But where's the missing link?"

I frowned. "It's got to be in there somewhere. This is driving me crazy."

Jacki and I were on the couch in my office. It was late Thursday afternoon. Eli Contini's defamation trial started the following Tuesday, and then Holly Goodman's murder trial was set for the following Monday.

But before shifting gears to the Contini case—something Jacki and I would do on Sunday—we were still puzzling over the mystery of Isaiah's murder. From the records we'd obtained—and especially the paperwork from the rejection of Holly's attempt to refinance the mortgage with one of the MP entities and the manuscript of Isaiah's autobiography—we'd established that all three members of Isaiah's inner circle—namely, Anna, Arnold Bell, and Mildred Haddock—had access to the photo of the cyanide containers in Holly's basement and had access to the manuscript with the personal details included in those three anonymous texts. And given that Alonzo Flynn was still at the mortgage company when the inspection report with the cyanide photos arrived and was later upstairs formatting the manuscript, he was our fourth candidate.

But access alone was not enough. We needed more. The missing link, as Jacki labeled it.

"The standard strategy," I said, "is to follow the money."

"Which leads us to Anna."

"His death sure made her wealthy." I frowned. "But still—she was pretty rich anyway."

"Not technically. He was her sugar daddy. As long as they stayed together, she'd be fine. But what if he dumped her?"

"True."

"Maybe she didn't want to move," Jacki said.

"What do you mean 'move'?"

"That stuff at the end of the manuscript."

"I haven't read that far."

"He ends the book—or I guess Glasscock ends it—with some New Age nonsense about closing that phase of his life and heading off into the sunset."

"Really?"

"It's all sort of frou-frou, but that's my interpretation. I'll get it." Jacki stood. "I printed it off. It's in my office."

She returned with the 276-page manuscript held together with a large binder clip. She plopped down on the couch beside me and flipped to the last page.

"Here," she said, handing me the manuscript and pointing to the last paragraphs.

I read:

And thus, midway on my life's journey, like another traveler centuries ago, I had found myself in the dark woods, the right road lost. But as you have read, I struggled to find my pathway through that inferno and into the purgatory of commerce, where I achieved great fame, prestige, and wealth.

But now I have reached the next stage in my epic

journey whence, guided by my own Beatrice, the lovely Anna, I shall leave purgatory behind and ascend to that paradise not of heaven but of this precious and fertile earth, where great opportunities await me.

Perhaps someday, dear reader, I shall share with you this closing chapter of my glorious saga.

Until then, I wish you health, good fortune, and tranquility.

I looked up at Jacki. "Really?"

She shrugged. "I guess so."

I looked down at that last page. "So his version of purgatory was his company. And he's going to leave it all behind?"

"Seems like it. What's with purgatory?"

"He must have read Dante's *Divine Comedy*. Or maybe Glasscock's a fan. That's the reference. But he says he's leaving it behind. That he's heading off to some heaven on earth. Where is that?"

Jacki smiled. "You're asking me?"

"This could be a big corporate issue. A huge one."

"Really?"

"Sure. He was the CEO of a major company. Even though he'd taken the company private, MP Enterprises had ongoing deals and transaction with lots of big companies, private and public. If this were disclosed—"

I paused.

"What?"

"I wonder if the company's lawyers knew about this?"

"What do you mean?"

"Jacki, think about it. I've seen a lot of business contracts— especially supply contracts—where a company like MP Enterprises would have to represent and warrant that it would promptly disclose any material change in management. Failure to disclose would give the other side the option to cancel the deal without liability. If the CEO was planning to leave the company, the lawyers would have to prepare and submit to all those other companies a detailed written notice laying out the transition plan."

"Okay?"

"Have we seen any such notice? Or even a draft?"

"Maybe he hadn't told them yet."

"Or maybe he had, and they were in the process of drafting the paperwork."

"Who are the company's lawyers?" she asked.

I smiled. "My old firm."

"Abbott & Windsor?"

"Yep."

"You think they'll tell you? Isn't that insider trading?"

"Not anymore. First, it's now a private company. And second, Isaiah's dead. He isn't going anywhere. At least not on this earth."

Jacki smiled. "True, and if that Dante guy is right, he's now in an awfully warm place."

Chapter Thirty

Friday.

The last weekday before final preparations for the trial of *Robb v. Contini*. But the topic at this brainstorming lunch at Mission Taco was the murder trial of Holly Goodman, scheduled to start the week after *Robb v. Contini*.

Benny took another bite of his burrito, downed it with a gulp of beer, and shook his head. "There's no such thing, Rachel."

"Maybe not in fiction, but it surely happens in real life."

"How so?" Jacki asked.

"Look at all the unsolved murders out there."

"That doesn't make them perfect murders," Jacki said. "Maybe it's just killers that got lucky."

"Or a homicide detective that fucked up," Benny said. "This ain't no episode of *CSI: St. Louis*, woman."

I was scheduled for two meetings on the murder case that afternoon—one at two with a corporate attorney at Abbott & Windsor, the firm that represents Isaiah's company, and the other at three thirty with Larry Glasscock, Isaiah's ghostwriter.

"Still, Benny," I said, "whoever did it managed to pull it off without leaving any clues."

"Other than clues that point to your client," Benny said.

The server arrived with a huge, messy *torta*—a shredded pork sandwich with smashed black beans, cheese, pickled onions, and chipotle bacon, all smothered in an ancho chili sauce.

The server—a young Latino—frowned as he looked at each of our plates. I still had one of my fish tacos, Jacki was working on the second of her three carne asada tacos, and Benny was only halfway through his burrito and hadn't yet touched his side of street corn fritters.

"The *torta ahogada*?" the server asked, apparently concerned he'd been sent to the wrong table.

I pointed at Benny. "Him."

Benny looked up from his burrito and nodded. "Extra bacon, right?"

"Yes, sir."

"Excellent, dude. Set her down right here. And"—he lifted his empty glass—"one more IPA, please."

Jacki and I exchanged glances.

"Tsk, tsk, ladies," Benny said, waving a finger at us. "Let she who has not sinned throw the first taco."

"Back to Holly's case," I said. "Getting the cyanide turns out to be not that hard. You can do it legitimately by showing a connection to some industry that uses it—and I assume MP Enterprises owns a few of those companies. Or you can also get it on the internet from a variety of online outfits, which I assume is what happened here. But that's the easy part. Think of that sequence of events. Everything had to work flawlessly for the killer to pull it off."

"Such as?" Benny said.

"The killer targeted Holly in advance, right? With those texts and the cyanide. But for the murder to work that day, Holly had to be in the room alone with him. More important, Isaiah had to be out of the room when she arrived."

"That's no surprise," Jacki said. "He made you wait when you went to his office, he made Megan wait in the conference room during the mediation, and then he made Holly wait. You told me you even warned them about the waiting. That was his little power game, right? His modus operandi. Make the other party sit there waiting for you because you're so damn important."

"True. But in addition to Isaiah being out of the room when she arrived, the poisoned coffee had to already be in there waiting for him to return."

Benny pointed at me with his burrito. "So?"

"C'mon, Benny. Too many ifs."

"Hey, the mediation date and location were set almost a month in advance. The photo of that cyanide was relatively recent, so the killer could assume the stuff was still in her basement. Even if it wasn't still there, you said yourself it wasn't that hard to obtain. And those three texts would be incriminating. Finally, the killer *knew* that Isaiah would make each sister wait, so there'd be plenty of time to sneak in the poisoned coffee while the conference room was empty. Just swap out the mug on the table for one with the poison."

We ate in silence for a few minutes.

"Another thing," Jacki said. "You're assuming this was the first time."

I frowned. "What do you mean?"

"If one of those four is the real killer, it's safe to assume that the idea of killing him didn't just pop up that day. Maybe this wasn't even the first time the killer tried to set up Isaiah's death. Maybe there was another time—or even two times—when those ifs didn't play out. Whether it was the first time or the fifth time, maybe the killer was willing to walk away if it didn't play out."

"Then why those texts?" I asked.

"Why not? I assume they were part of the plan, but they wouldn't backfire even if the killer abandoned the plan. Sure, they'd make Isaiah furious, make him blame his sisters, and make him even less willing to settle with them. But why would the killer care about that? Heck, it might even open up another opportunity to kill him."

"She's got a point," Benny said. "There's gotta be a gambler in every killer. You keep folding 'til you draw a winning hand."

I thought it over. "So you think this wasn't the first time?"

Jacki shrugged. "We'll never know, but it's possible. Sometimes the stars align, Rachel, sometimes they don't."

"Well, we know one thing for certain: the killer had a good plan, right down to using that burner phone for the texts to Isaiah's phone."

"Actually…" Benny popped a street corn fritter into his mouth and scratched his neck as he chewed. "That burner phone might be worth checking out."

"We did," Jacki said. "Assuming the killer paid for it with cash—a safe assumption—there's no way to connect a name to that phone."

"True," Benny said, "but that doesn't necessarily end the inquiry."

"What do you mean?" I asked.

"I was talking the other day with Rob Steinbrook. He's one of the profs at Wash U. Teaches criminal law. We got on the topic of burner cell phones. Some recent Supreme Court due process case. Anyway, turns out that if you can figure out the wireless carrier—you know, like Verizon or Sprint—you can often get at least a general location for where a call was made. Or a text was sent. And if you can figure out the carrier for the recipient of the call, you can apparently get a pretty good fix on that location. That won't get you the name of the caller, but sometimes the location can be almost as good."

Jacki and I looked at each other, eyebrows raised.

I turned back to Benny. "But how do you figure out the carrier?"

"Apparently, it's not that hard. Sometimes just a Google search of the number will give you the wireless carrier. I think the technical term is 'mobile network carrier.'"

I turned back to Jacki. "We have the phone number for that burner."

She nodded. "And we already know the wireless carrier for Isaiah's phone."

"Yep."

Jacki gave me a wink. "I'm on it. Right after lunch."

I turned to Benny. "Thank you, Sherlock Holmes."

"Elementary, my dear Rachel."

I pointed at the huge *torta* that Benny had just lifted with both hands. "What's that monstrosity called?"

"This epicurean delight is known as the ahogada."

"Save room for more, Professor. The next one's on me."

"Awesome!"

Chapter Thirty-One

Billy Brice and I met as junior associates at Abbott & Windsor—Billy in the St. Louis office (which numbered fifteen lawyers back then), me in the Chicago office (which then numbered about two hundred fifty lawyers). I was in the firm's litigation group, spending most of my time on massive antitrust cases. Billy was in the firm's corporate group, doing whatever junior associates in that group in St. Louis did back then.

That was more than a decade ago. I am now a partner in the two-lawyer firm of Gold & Brand, and Billy Brice is now William H. Brice III, a partner in the Corporate Finance and Securities Group at Abbott & Windsor (which now has more than 1,500 lawyers worldwide). But he's still Billy Brice to me—and drawing upon our mutual St. Louis origins (at rival high schools, in fact), I convinced him to meet me "off campus" at Café Ventana, a coffeehouse near St. Louis University.

He arrived looking every inch the young partner at an international law firm: gray pinstriped suit, white Oxford shirt, navy tie, black cap-toe shoes, and a cell phone pressed against his ear. He spotted me at my table and waved.

We hadn't seen each other in almost ten years—and Billy had gained some weight since then, although those added pounds appeared to be evenly enough distributed to make him look just thicker than I remembered instead of downright fat. His face had always been round with red cheeks. It was a tad rounder now, the cheeks still flushed. As before, he still wore his curly blond hair cut short, though the hairline had moved an inch or two higher on his forehead. In short, he was still immediately recognizable—the big, burly guy with the friendly demeanor.

"Understood, John," he said on the phone as he pulled out the chair opposite me. "I'll have someone look into that today and we'll get back to you first thing tomorrow. Okay? Gotta go, man. Talk soon."

He ended the call and gave me a big smile as he slid the phone into the inside pocket on his suit jacket.

"Hello, Rachel. Wow, it's been awhile, eh?"

"I'll say. I knew you when you were just Billy. You're a big shot now."

He laughed. "Big shot? I think I'm talking to the big shot at this table."

"Yeah, right." I stood. "I'm going to get a latte. What can I get you?"

"I can get it."

"Sit. I'm the one who asked for this meeting. My treat."

He gave me a salute. "Yes, ma'am. We all learned a long time ago not to get crossways with Rachel Gold. Let's see...well, I'll have a latte, too. Thanks."

He was back on the phone when I returned with our two lattes but ended the call as I placed his cup and saucer before him.

"Ah, nice. Thanks, Rachel."

"My pleasure."

He took a sip and leaned back in his chair. "Okay. Tell me what's up."

"MP Enterprises."

He nodded, eyes narrowing. "Okay. As you probably know, we represent them on corporate matters."

"That's why we're here, Billy."

"Then you know I'm bound by the attorney-client privilege."

"I do. And my goal is to talk about something outside the scope of that privilege."

He gave me a dubious look. "Okay."

I took a sip of my latte. "I assume you had dealings with the company's late chairman and CEO."

"I did."

"Did you know he hired a freelance writer to help him write his autobiography?"

Billy's eyes widened. "Really? I had no idea."

"I read the manuscript. Guess how it ends?"

Billy shrugged. "No clue."

I opened my notepad, took out my photocopy of the last two pages of the manuscript, and read him the final paragraphs—the part about having decided to leave the purgatory of commerce and "ascend to the paradise not of heaven but of this precious and fertile earth."

I looked up. "Well?"

Billy frowned. "Well?"

"If I understand that final passage correctly, Billy, Isaiah was planning to exit MP Enterprises and move on to something very different."

Billy nodded, lips pursed. "Okay."

"And if the chairman and CEO of MP Enterprises had an exit plan, especially one that was imminent, I assume that the company would need to file appropriates notices with all the companies that did business with MP Enterprises."

He took a sip of his latte and set the cup down on the saucer. "Okay."

"I did a little poking around. Guess what?"

"What?"

"No such notices."

"That is correct."

"So what's the deal, Billy?"

"What do you mean?"

"If he was planning to leave the company—if he told you his plans—why wasn't your firm preparing the notice?"

Billy frowned. "Rachel, you're pushing the boundaries here."

"No, I'm not. If he were still alive, sure. But whether he was planning to leave the company back then, he's certainly gone now. And he ain't coming back. And meanwhile I'm defending the woman accused of killing him. She's innocent, Billy. I am certain of that. I think someone in the company killed him."

"What? In the company?"

"Yes, and I'm looking for a motive to kill him beside the fact that he was an obnoxious self-centered jerk."

Billy smiled. "Well, he certainly was that. His Rule Number One for any lawyer representing his company was that you had to have your cell phone turned on and sitting on your nightstand every night, even if you were out of town on vacation. I can't add up the number of times he woke me in the wee hours with some issue that could easily have waited until the morning. It got so bad that my wife started sleeping in the guest room."

He chuckled as he shook his head.

"Frankly, his death was at least a plus in the Brice household. I have my wife back in bed with me."

"So was he planning to leave the company?"

Billy took another sip of his latte as he considered his response. "Well, yes and no."

He gestured toward my notepad. "This is confidential, Rachel. Understand?"

"I do."

"Okay. The answer is maybe."

"Maybe? He's dead, Billy. If his departure was going to hurt the company's value or its deals with other companies, that's already happened. There's nothing left to disclose."

"Well..." He frowned as he moved his head back and forth.

"Possibly. He was actually working on something that we were planning to disclose, but that fell apart when he died."

"So that deal is dead?"

Billy nodded.

"What was it?"

"You are correct about Isaiah's plans. He did want out. I assumed he wanted to leave St. Louis—and take along his girl-friend, that one-named gal."

"Anna?"

"Yeah, that's her." He shook his head. "Another piece of work."

"Go on."

"He'd been in preliminary talks with this foreign outfit. A big investment firm out of South America. I won't name them, but they have a reputation for acquiring companies like MP Enterprises and then making massive cost cuts and selling off underperforming subsidiaries. They've had great success with that business model over the years. The shareholders of those companies are usually happy but the remaining executives, and there are rarely many that survive the transition, are miserable. Anyway, Isaiah's idea was to sell them MP Enterprises. We never got beyond preliminary deal terms, though."

I jotted down a note. "What happened?"

"He died, and so did the deal. That company sent formal notice three days later that they were terminating all discussions."

I nodded. "So nothing to disclose."

"Exactly."

"Who else at MP Enterprises knew about the discussions?"

Billy rubbed his chin. "Probably most of the top execs. That would be maybe five or six besides Isaiah, although most of them had only the vaguest details. Probably someone in accounting and some-one in IT. I assume they all had to sign nondisclosure agreements."

"Did Anna know?"

Billy nodded. "Definitely. She was in several of our meetings with Isaiah."

"What about Arnold Bell?"

"Probably. He wasn't in the actual meetings, but he was involved in gathering materials for us that were related to the possible transaction."

"What kind of materials?"

"Research data on the potential buyer. Internal finance numbers. Hierarchies within the various subsidiaries."

"What about Isaiah's assistant?"

"Do you mean his secretary?"

"Mildred Haddock. I'm not sure of her title."

"I'm sure she knew. Isaiah dictated his notes and memos on the deal issues, and she's the one who typed them up for him."

I checked off their names on my notepad. "So the deal is dead."

Billy nodded. "As a doornail."

"Did Isaiah tell you what he planned to do after the sale?"

"Nothing specific. All I know is that he was going to be a wealthy man."

"He was already."

"True, but if the deal went through he was going to receive more than two hundred million dollars for his shares of the company's stock."

"Did he say he was going to move from St. Louis?"

Billy frowned as he tried to remember. "I assumed that was part of his plan, but I can't say for sure he told me that. He never shared any personal details with me. That wasn't his style—at least with his company lawyers."

I mulled that over as I jotted down a note. I looked up at Billy. "His *company* lawyers, you said. Did he have personal lawyers?"

"I assume he did."

"Did you ever communicate with any of them?"

Billy frowned as he weighed his response. "Not directly."

"What does that mean?"

"Why do you ask, Rachel? Does that really matter?"

"It might, and it might not. I'm defending an innocent woman,

Billy, which means I have to turn over every stone I can find. For example, are you aware he was renting a one-bedroom apartment near his office? From what we can tell, the purported tenant was a fake LLC."

"I did not know that."

"He apparently used it for sex. But not with Anna."

"Okay, but the same question. Why would that matter?"

"It's just another example of his bogus character. There was the public Isaiah and the private Isaiah, and they don't sync up."

"We both know that's not unusual, Rachel."

"Agreed. I'm just trying to probe a little deeper into the private Isaiah. I was surprised to learn about that secret apartment, although I guess I shouldn't have been. Anyone who engineers a hostile takeover of his own father's company is capable of anything. So, I'm asking you, Billy, can you think of anything you learned about his private life that seemed noteworthy?"

Billy leaned back in his chair and gazed at me. "This is confidential. Deal?"

"Depends, Billy. The man is dead. Just tell me and let me take it from there."

"Okay. So in doing our due diligence on that South American deal, we had several associates and paralegals reviewing hundreds of thousands of documents, both ours and theirs. They happened to come across a file in the MP documents labeled 'Mossack Fonseca.'"

"Mossack Fonseca." The name was vaguely familiar. "What is it?"

"Was, not is. Remember that Panama Papers scandal? Mossack Fonseca was the law firm at the center of that controversy. Someone somehow released millions of that firm's confidential documents. Those are the ones that detailed how the rich and powerful around the world used offshore accounts to avoid billions in taxes. Those rich folks were Mossack Fonseca's clients. The firm created their offshore accounts and managed all that money. The leaked documents and the bad publicity destroyed the firm. They ended up closing down."

"Isaiah was one of their clients?"

Billy nodded.

"I guess I'm not shocked." I made a note. "How did that particular file end up in the company documents?"

"Apparently, it was misfiled. It should have been in his personal documents."

"So did it show how much money he had offshore?"

"It did. It was a lot of money." He paused. "But that's not what struck me about the file."

I looked up from my notes. "Tell me."

Billy took another sip of his latte and set the cup down. He stared at it for a moment and then looked at me. "Isaiah stayed in touch with one of the Panama lawyers after the firm collapsed. The folder contained a confidential memorandum to Isaiah. It was dated about a month after the start of the discussions with that South American company. The memo was in response to Isaiah's request for certain information."

"What kind of information?"

"He'd asked for a list of countries without extradition treaties with the United States that were friendly and safe for American expatriots."

I stared at Billy. "For American expats?"

He nodded.

"Did the memo describe the reason for his concern?"

"No."

"Wow. Do you remember the countries recommended?"

He squinted as he tilted his head toward the ceiling.

"A few." He lowered his gaze. "Obviously, there were plenty of nonstarters—countries like Bangladesh, Rwanda, Cambodia, Russia. But I do remember the memo included a few safe spots that, oddly enough, all started with the letter M."

"Such as?"

"There was Madagascar and the Maldives. I think Montenegro was in there. Maybe Morocco. Mozambique was on the list. I can't remember any others."

I jotted down the countries. "But you have no idea why he wanted that information?"

"None. But I confess it was a little unsettling, especially while we were in the middle of negotiating that deal with the potential purchaser."

"What did you do?"

"Ultimately, nothing. I was tempted to ask him about it, Rachel. But the file was clearly supposed to be a confidential personal file, not a company file, which meant I wasn't supposed to know about it. So I stayed mum."

"You never found out anything more? Any reason why he wanted that information."

"I didn't. And whatever he was contemplating died with him."

I scribbled another note in my notepad. "You said earlier that his girlfriend, Anna, was a piece of work."

"Oh, yeah."

"How so?"

"Oh, man." He shook his head. "She reminded me of my sixth-grade teacher, Miss Hanson."

"Really?"

"Miss Hanson was strict and mean. She never smiled, never said anything nice to any of us, and got angry over little things. That's Anna. I don't think I ever saw her smile, and she had a nasty way of asking questions during the meetings. Very intimidating— and not just to me. You could see she had that effect on the others in those meetings. On everyone but Isaiah. She gave me the creeps."

Chapter Thirty-Two

Larry Glasscock stroked his thick walrus mustache with his thumb and index finger as he weighed his answer.

"That was a touchy subject," he finally said.

"How so?"

"They didn't agree."

"On the move?"

"Yes, on the move."

I was in Glasscock's apartment, which is where we'd met the first time. And, as before, he had on a wrinkled white shirt, black sweater vest, baggy gray dress slacks, and white tennis shoes.

"The manuscript seemed kind of vague at the end," I said.

"That's how he wanted me to leave it. Kind of vague. No destination. Just some nebulous reference to a paradise on the earth."

"Had he picked that paradise?"

"Yes and no."

"What does that mean?"

"When we first discussed the matter, he had his paradise selected. Or so he told me."

"What was it?"

"Bend."

"Pardon."

"Bend, Oregon. Actually, somewhere just outside of Bend. I never got the specific location."

"Had he visited there?"

"So he claimed. He bought some property there—or at least that's what he told me. I don't know if there was a house there or he was going to build one. I didn't pry. All I knew was that it was confidential and I couldn't tell a soul. He made that crystal clear."

"But Anna didn't want to move there?"

Glasscock shrugged. "That's what he said. She sat in on one of our interviews, but this came up in a later meeting with just the two of us. He said she was adamant that she would never move. He claimed he'd be able to change her mind but that it might take a while."

I jotted *Bend?* on my notepad and looked up at him.

"When I asked if he'd picked his paradise, you said yes and no. What does the no mean?"

"I'm not sure." Glasscock shook his head. "In a later meeting I was trying to get a little more information for the book's final chapter. I asked him something general about Bend, about whether he'd started building a house out there and whether Anna had changed her mind. He got really mad. He told me to forget about Bend and forget about Anna. I was kind of flustered. I tried to apologize. He just waved it away and changed the subject."

"Did he ever say anything about leaving the country?"

"You mean moving to some other country?"

"Yes."

Glasscock leaned back in his chair and frowned. "Did he ever say anything about leaving the country? Not directly."

"What does that mean?"

"Again, I'm not sure. The last time we met he was actually in a good mood. That was unusual. When his secretary showed me into his office, he was playing music over the speakers. 'Remember this song?' he asked me. I did."

"What was it?"

"An old Crosby, Stills & Nash song. 'Marrakesh Express.'"

"Okay."

"And guess what was on his desk?"

"What?"

"Some sort of real estate brochure. It was open to this full-page color photo of a truly luxurious villa with palm trees and a swimming pool. Magnificent. He caught me staring at it. He actually smiled, like he was proud. 'Marrakesh?' I asked him. Well, he closed the brochure, put it in his desk drawer, and gave me one of his glares. None of my business, he told me. Said the entire topic was off limits. Strictly confidential. I couldn't tell a soul. No one. Period. Did I understand? I told him I did."

"Was that villa in Marrakesh?"

Glasscock shrugged. "I think I recall seeing the word Morocco on that page but I can't be sure."

"Did Anna know about that?"

"I have no idea."

I wrote *Marrakesh?* on my notepad.

"Did he talk to you about his company?" I asked. "About what was going to happen when he left?"

"Again, he was kind of vague. He mentioned selling it to some foreign outfit, but he wouldn't give me any details."

"Did he say what he was planning to do when he sold the company and left St. Louis?"

Glasscock shook his head. "Not clearly, that's for sure. Back when he was moving to Bend, or said he was, it sounded like some sort of spiritual thing. Or maybe religious. Kind of—if you don't mind my saying so—a hippie-dippie kind of tantric sort of thing. Pretty vague. Don't get me wrong. He sounded like he was committed. I just didn't grasp what it was, and he wouldn't give me any details. And maybe he was bullshitting me, especially after he told me to forget about Bend. Not that it mattered, because I couldn't put it in the book anyway. But it certainly didn't sound like he was planning on a new business venture."

"But Anna wasn't on board. Even after Bend?"

"Apparently not."

"Did Arnold Bell know about any of this?"

Glasscock tugged at his mustache. "Good question. I can't say for sure. Arnold seemed to know all kinds of things over there, professional and personal, but I don't know about the Oregon stuff or Morocco or whatever he was planning."

"What about Isaiah's secretary, Miss Haddock?"

"Same answer. Don't know. But keep in mind that she handled all his travel stuff, so if he was going out to Oregon or somewhere else to look at property, she would have known. She would have made the flight arrangements, booked him a hotel, rented him a car."

"Same with Morocco?"

"I suppose so, if he was serious about it." He raised his eyebrows. "That Haddock woman is one formidable lady."

"Agreed."

He chuckled. "I learned to steer clear of both of those women—Anna and Haddock." He paused and gazed at me. "And you should, too."

———

I sat in my car outside Glasscock's apartment, the engine idling, sorting through what I'd learned from him and from Billy Brice, struggling to find a way to fit the puzzle pieces together. Morocco? We'd probably never know the answer. Whatever he was planning died with him.

Eventually, I shifted the engine into Drive, pulled away from the curb, and tried to focus on happier thoughts. Sam and I were going to Abe's house tonight for Shabbos dinner with Abe and his girls. I was bringing the challah, which I'd baked late last night as I listened to Joni Mitchell and tried not to obsess over my next two weeks. It was hard enough preparing for one trial, but with two back-to-back, I felt like my head was going to explode.

Still, tonight would be nice, and Saturday was going to be my Sam day. All day. The zoo in the morning, Crown Candy Kitchen for lunch, the Magic House in the afternoon, and somewhere fun for pizza at night.

And then my mother, God bless her, would take over all household chores and Sam duties through both trials.

Oy.

THE CIRCUIT COURT OF

THE CITY OF ST. LOUIS

(22nd Judicial Circuit)

STATE OF MISSOURI

Tuesday Docket

Division K: Judge LaDonna Williams

Trial Setting (non-jury)—9:00 a.m.

Cecilia E. Robb v. Eli Contini,

Case No. 1792-CC09A227

Chapter Thirty-Three

"Well?" Jacki said.

I stepped back, crossing my arms as I studied the poster. It was a blow-up of a color photograph of two cars parked side by side on a wide circular driveway. The car on the left was a silver Corvette. The car on the right was a silver Mercedes-Benz coupe with gold trim. An ornate Spanish-tile mailbox was visible in the left foreground with the address stenciled in gold: #6 Sienna. Looming above the cars in the background was the twenty-one-thousand-square-foot Mission-style home of Rich and Cissy Robb. The vanity plate on the silver Corvette read I'M RICH. The vanity plate on the Mercedes read ME, TOO.

I looked over at Jacki and nodded. "I like it. I like it a lot."

She reached for her trial exhibit stickers and turned to me. "Mark it?"

"Yep. Exhibit H, right?"

"Right."

It was eight thirty on Monday night. The trial started the following morning. We were at my office doing the usual last-minute preparations: marking trial exhibits, making copies of key documents, outlining direct examinations, making notes for cross-examination. Benny had dropped by to help. He was in a chair in the corner reading through a pile of recent libel decisions in an effort to breathe some life into Eli Contini's affirmative defenses.

I watched as Jacki peeled off the back of the exhibit sticker and carefully affixed it to the upper right corner of the poster. The sticker read DEFENDANT'S TRIAL EXHIBIT H.

"Okay," I said. "We'll need to wrap it and mark it on the outside."

I pointed to the other poster. "Let's make this Exhibit I."

"Got it."

I turned to the third poster, which was already wrapped in plain brown paper and sealed with tape. "Which makes this one, Exhibit J."

I bent down, removed the cap from the marker, and printed DEFENDANT'S TRIAL EXHIBIT J across the brown paper. I straightened up, replaced the cap on the marker, and stepped back to admire my handiwork.

Benny looked up from his cases and shook his head. "Let's hope you never have to unwrap that present, Hanukah Jo."

"Agreed."

"Does your client know about Exhibit J?" Benny asked.

"Oh, no. He's nervous enough as it is."

Benny slowly shook his head. "Holy shit, Rachel. This isn't Texas Hold'em"

"Think about it, Benny. Why else would her creepy husband threaten me?"

"Because he's a total asshole."

"True, but still, why? He even vaguely suggested he might pay Eli some money if we agreed to end the case. Money? My client is the *defendant*, not the plaintiff. So why? I'm thinking he's worried for his wife. Maybe worried we might be able to prove she wore that dress. And if he was the one who told her to return the dress, he might be even more worried about having to face her after the trial."

"Possibly," Benny said. "But the way he acted that day in the park, with that thug of his standing behind him, I think it's more likely he's just a prick accustomed to intimidating people, especially women. Meanwhile"—Benny looked over at Jacki—"what's your take on Exhibit J?"

She shuddered. "I don't want to think about it."

Benny turned back to me. "You sure about this?"

"Of course not. I admit it's a little risky."

"A *little* risky? Are you fucking kidding me, Rachel? Bringing that into the courtroom is like playing a round of Russian Roulette."

"Let's hope not." I forced a smile. "I'd prefer to think of it as... well, truth in a plain brown wrapper."

Jacki laughed. "I like that."

"Tell you what, gorgeous," Benny said. "you walk out of that courtroom unharmed and we're heading straight over to the Casino Queen and betting it all on red."

Chapter Thirty-Four

At 9:05 the next morning, I rose at counsel's table. Eli Contini was seated next to me, ramrod straight, his hands steepled beneath his chin.

"Defendant is ready," I announced.

Judge LaDonna Williams nodded gravely. "We'll start in a moment."

She leaned over and said something to her docket clerk, who got to her feet and came around behind the bench to confer with the judge. As they talked in hushed tones, I turned toward the gallery, which was usually empty save for one or two elderly court-watchers. Today, though, a crowd of two dozen was scattered along the benches. I recognized the society correspondent and the gossip columnist for the *Post-Dispatch*, seated side by side in the third row. Behind them was a reporter from Channel Five with a steno pad open on her lap. One row over was Charles Morley, the photographer from the *Post-Dispatch*—here today not as a spectator but as a witness. Jacki had served him with a trial subpoena. I caught his eye and smiled. He acknowledged me with a nod. I spotted two other witnesses we'd subpoenaed. With any luck this morning, they'd never have to take the stand.

Seated in the first row directly behind us were Eli Contini's stout wife, Dorothy, and their stouter son, Gabriel. Gabriel had Down's syndrome. He was in his thirties and had an angelic disposition. I winked at Dorothy Contini, who nodded nervously. Gabriel smiled and gave me a thumbs-up.

On the other side of the courtroom, in the first row behind plaintiff's table, sat Richie Robb, the CEO of Pacific Rim Industries and, of course, the creepy husband of the plaintiff. Richie was flanked by two members of his entourage—although neither one was the thug he'd brought with him to the park that day. In contrast to his grim lieutenants, however, Richie seemed almost languid this morning. With his heavy-lidded eyes, shiny black suit, and slicked-back hair, he reminded me of a drowsy well-fed panther.

"Counsel," Judge Williams said, peering down at us over her reading glasses, "I've read your trial briefs and I'm familiar with your legal theories. We'll dispense with opening statements."

She turned to my opponent. "Mr. Brenner, call your first witness."

"Thank you so much, Your Honor," Howard Brenner said in his toadying manner.

He turned to his client, who was seated next to him. With a sweeping gesture, he announced, "Your Honor, we call the plaintiff herself, Mrs. Cecelia Robb."

She rose with steely poise and strode across the courtroom to the witness box, where the clerk was waiting. Today she wore a subdued but elegant red wool suit and matching neck scarf that brought out the highlights in her shoulder-length auburn hair.

"Please raise your right hand," the clerk told her.

And thus the trial began.

Many who knew Cissy Robb claimed that she had ice in her veins. Just last year, for example, she'd refused to pay her ten-thousand-dollar pledge to the St. Louis Special Olympics when, instead of being seated for the luncheon at the *A* table (with guest of honor Celine Dion and the wives of several St. Louis

CEOs), she found herself at a table that included two of the gold medal winners at the day's competition. As she informed the chairwoman of the event, "I didn't pledge ten grand to eat lunch with a pair of retards."

Perhaps to soften her image, Howard Brenner started his examination slow and gentle—marital status, children, pets, hobbies. I glanced over at Richie, who had momentarily perked up when his wife took the stand. He soon lost interest, though, and turned to one of his assistants to whisper something. The assistant nodded intently, jumped to his feet, and scurried out of the courtroom. Richie turned with a bored expression to watch him leave. As he turned back, our eyes briefly met. He stared at me as he raised his middle finger to scratch his nose. Then he glanced down at his cell phone.

While Cissy's social aspirations might never quite surmount her husband's crudeness, I conceded that the woman had resolve. Looking at her seated in the witness box, elegantly groomed and perfectly coifed, it was obvious that the former Charlotte Gutterman was breathing thinner air these days.

We were now nearly an hour into Brenner's warm and cuddly preliminaries about her background and family. Finally, he reached the day that Cissy labeled, in a halting voice, Black Tuesday.

"Tell us about it," he said, oozing with faux compassion.

What followed was a performance deserving of a Tony nomination. We heard about her initial confusion when Eli Contini responded with a silent scowl to her request to return the dress. Then the embarrassment of having him place the dress under a high-intensity lamp and inspecting it with a magnifying glass. Then the dismay of struggling to maintain her composure while he fired questions at her, his voice "literally dripping with hostility." And finally, the mortification of public disgrace.

"There were other women in there," she said, her lips quivering, "Women I know—women I admire—women I respect."

She paused to dab her eye with a handkerchief. "He raised his voice to me. He was practically shouting at me. He called me a liar and he called me a cheat. Those women heard every one of his vile accusations."

She paused and took a deep breath, her face contorted in anguish.

Brenner, oozing more faux compassion, asked, "Was it painful, Cissy?"

She sighed, her hands fluttering helplessly onto her lap. "Oh, you have no idea."

"Please tell the Court, Cissy."

As if on cue—indeed, on cue—she covered her face with her hands and began sobbing.

Brenner winced in what I assumed was his attempt to portray empathy. After a few seconds, Judge Williams quietly announced that the court would be in short recess.

Brenner helped his client off the stand and walked her out of the courtroom. Richie, huddling near the back of the courtroom with his two aides, glanced over at his wife as Brenner escorted her out. When the door closed, he turned back to his aides and said something that made them laugh.

Chapter Thirty-Five

I used the break to get my exhibits arranged. Brenner had to know that he couldn't top that last scene. His expression confirmed as much when he strolled back into the courtroom alone. He could not have looked more pleased with his performance that morning.

"Rachel," he said, with a phony sympathetic smile, "I am sorry to inform you that our last settlement offer is off the table."

I nodded.

Five minutes later, with his restored and composed client back on the witness stand, Howard Brenner stood to announce, "No further questions, Your Honor."

He turned to me with a smug bow. "Your witness, Counsel."

I checked my watch as I stood.

11:15 am.

We'd break for lunch around noon, which gave me forty-five minutes to set it up. So far, things were going according to the plan—namely, the one I'd worked out in the wee hours last night. If my plan worked, the case would end over the lunch hour. If it didn't, well, we'd be stuck in a high-stakes mud-wrestling match for at least another day and a half.

I came around counsel's table to face her.

"Good morning, Mrs. Robb," I said in a polite voice. "My name is Rachel Gold and I represent the defendant."

She nodded, her eyes chilly.

"I have a few questions for you, but before I ask them I would like to make sure I understand your claim."

I moved back over to Eli Contini and put my hand on his shoulder. "You have sued my client for libel. You claim he said some defamatory things about you, right?"

She looked from me to Contini and then back to me.

"That is correct." She sounded annoyed by the question.

"In fact, you allege that Mr. Contini said you were lying about whether you wore the dress. You allege that he accused you of trying to cheat him by asking for a full refund on something that you had already used."

Her nostrils flared. "That is precisely what he said."

"And to be clear, you allege here that his accusations were false, correct?"

She gave me an imperious stare. "Correct. And I don't simply allege that. They *were* lies."

"In fact, Mrs. Robb, you allege that you didn't wear that dress at all, correct?"

"It's not an allegation," she snapped. "It's the truth."

"Thank you." I nodded at her. "I believe you have made your position clear."

I walked over to the wall hook where the dress hung, tagged with an exhibit sticker, and turned to face her.

"I would like us to go back to last summer. Tuesday, August eleventh, to be specific. That was the day you bought this lovely Oscar de la Renta gown from Mr. Contini, right?"

"Yes."

"According to the receipt, you paid $10,925.43 for that gown, correct?"

"Yes."

"You bought two more expensive clothing items the next day, right?"

She shrugged indifferently. "I'm sure I don't remember something that far back."

I smiled politely.

"I understand completely, Mrs. Robb. I can't even remember what I had for breakfast today. Let's see if we can jog your memory."

I spent the next fifteen minutes refreshing her recollection with charge receipts, credit slips, and her credit card bill for that period in August. When I finished, Cissy found herself cautiously eyeing Defendant's Trial Exhibits E and F, which were resting on the ledge of the witness box directly in front of her. Exhibit E was the pair of Manolo Blahnik black pumps that she had purchased for $920.67 on August 12. Exhibit F was the Salvatore Ferragamo handbag that she had purchased for $1,750.35 on the same day.

"Let's make sure our dates are correct," I said, turning to the blackboard. "On Tuesday you bought that pretty dress. On Wednesday you bought the matching pumps and purse. Then, on the following Tuesday, after the weekend, you returned the purse to Neiman Marcus and the shoes to La Femme Elegànte."

I turned and gave her my perky kindergarten teacher smile. "Right?"

She frowned at the blackboard and then looked down at the receipts already admitted into evidence as trial exhibits. "I suppose."

"Is that a yes, Mrs. Robb?"

She looked at me, her eyes narrowing. "Yes," she hissed.

Another perky smile. "I thought so."

I walked back toward counsel's table. I sat against the table edge, facing the witness, and crossed my arms over my chest. "Tell us about the night of August fourteenth. It was the Friday of the week you bought the dress and the shoes and the purse."

She laughed. "Get serious. That was months ago. I have no idea what I did that night."

Leaning across the table, I lifted the next exhibit off the pile. "Let's see if we can refresh that memory of yours again."

I walked over to the witness box. "Mrs. Robb, I am handing you what I have marked Defendant's Trial Exhibit G."

I gave an extra copy to the judge and one to Brenner.

Turning back to the witness, no warmth in my voice now. "Identify it, Mrs. Robb."

She stared at the document for a moment and then looked over at Howard Brenner with a frown.

"Identify Exhibit G," I repeated, turning toward Brenner. He dropped his eyes.

Carefully, slowly, she said, "It appears to be a program."

"A program for what?"

"It appears to be a program for a fund-raiser."

"Specifically, the program for the Carousel Auction Gala sponsored by the Friends of the Children's Hospital, correct?"

Fortunately, the Ritz-Carlton had kept several copies of the program.

She shrugged, trying to sound offhand. "That's what it says."

"What's the date of the event?"

She looked at the program. "According to this thing, August fourteenth."

"According to that thing?" I repeated, incredulous. "You can surely do better than that, can't you, Mrs. Robb? You attended that event, correct?"

She sat back with a frown, as if trying to remember. "I might have. I go to many charity events. Fund-raisers, galas, that sort of thing. My husband and I are very generous. We support many worthy causes. It's one of our passions. As for this one"—she gestured toward the program—"I can't recall for sure."

"Let me help you, then. Let's see if we can jog that foggy memory of yours."

Brenner leaped to his feet. "I object, Your Honor. Such derogatory language is disgraceful."

Judge Williams peered down at me over her reading glasses. "Sustained. Easy on the adjectives, Miss Gold."

"Your Honor," Brenner said, pausing for a toadying smile, "perhaps this would be a good time for a break."

I glanced at the clock. Ten minutes to twelve.

"Judge," I said, "could I at least conclude this line of questioning? It won't take long, and then we can start on a new line after lunch."

Judge Williams nodded. "Proceed, Counsel."

I turned to Cissy, who was eyeing me warily. "Open that program to page five, Mrs. Robb."

As she flipped to that page, I was pleased to see that Judge Williams had also turned to the same page of her copy of the program.

"Do you see the list of committee members for the event, Mrs. Robb? Look in the second column, sixth name down. That's your name, right?"

"Yes," she said with a trace of disdain, "but that doesn't prove anything. I serve on committees for many worthwhile causes. That doesn't mean I have time to attend every single one of their events."

"Now turn to page three."

She did. The Judge did. Howard Brenner did.

"You see that list of featured auction items? Do you see the fourth item? What is it?"

She looked up slowly, sensing for the first time that maybe, just maybe, she'd wandered into dangerous territory. "A Corvette."

I turned to my client. "Mr. Contini, could you please place Exhibit H on the easel?"

All eyes in the courtroom watched him walk over to the side wall, where three poster-sized objects wrapped in brown paper leaned against the wall. The first one was marked in bold black marker DEFENDANT'S EXHIBIT H. He brought it over and set it up on the easel facing the witness box and Judge Williams. Brenner got up and came around to watch.

"Mrs. Robb," I said, turning to her, "take a look at what I've marked Defendant's Trial Exhibit H."

I glanced over at Eli Contini and nodded. He reached up and tore the brown wrapping off the poster board, revealing the enlarged side-by-side shot of the two cars in the Robbs' driveway. I leaned back on the edge of the table, rested my hands on the table, and waited.

Behind me in the gallery you could hear some whispering and muffled voices.

Cissy stared intently at the photo, her brows knitted in concentration. You could almost hear the neurons firing. Eventually, she shifted her gaze to me.

"I remember now," she said with a frosty smile. "My husband and I attended that function."

"As a matter of fact, you bought the Corvette there, didn't you?"

She gave me a haughty look. "We didn't simply *buy* that car, Miss Gold. We acquired it in exchange for a very generous donation to a very worthy cause."

I couldn't help but smile. Might as well take a freebie.

"A very worthy cause," I repeated as I came over to the witness box and removed the program from the stand. Leafing through the program as I returned to counsel's table, I said, "And what exactly was that...very worthy cause?"

Silence.

I kept my back to her, waiting.

Five seconds.

Ten seconds.

"Objection," Brenner said, scrambling to his feet. "Irrelevant."

Someone in the gallery chuckled. I glanced up just as the gossip columnist for the *Post-Dispatch* started whispering to the society columnist, who smiled and nodded.

I turned back toward the court. I'd already scored the point, as was clear from Judge Williams' efforts to keep a straight face.

"I'll withdraw the question, Your Honor."

I turned to my client. "Mr. Contini, could you bring over Exhibit I?"

He walked back to the side wall and fetched the second wrapped poster. This one had DEFENDANT'S EXHIBIT I printed in bold black letters on the brown paper.

I turned to the witness. "Do you recall the article on the charity event in that Sunday's *Post-Dispatch*?"

Cissy glanced uncertainly at her attorney and then back at me.

I sighed patiently. "Okay, let's see if we can refresh that memory again."

I nodded at Eli Contini. He tore off the wrapping paper, revealing the blow-up of the society column from the "Style Plus" section of the Sunday, August 16 edition of the *Post-Dispatch*. This is one that Jacki had found for me. The blow-up included the photograph of two women standing in front of a carousel horse.

I pointed to the caption beneath the photograph. "Do you see this photo credit down here?"

Cissy leaned forward. "Uh, yes."

"Charles Morley," I read aloud.

I turned to her. "Do you remember Mr. Morley?"

Uneasy, she shook her head. "I don't think so."

"He's in the courtroom."

I turned toward the gallery.

"Charles," I called, "please hold up your hand."

Self-consciously, Morley raised his hand.

I turned back to Cissy.

"Remember him, Mrs. Robb? He was there that night. For over an hour. Walking around among the guests, taking photographs." I paused. "*Lots* of photographs."

Her eyes darted between the photographer and me. "I—I don't remember."

More whispers and muffled buzz from the gallery.

"Really?" I gave her a look of mild disbelief. "You don't remember him taking *lots* of photographs?"

Cissy looked at Brenner. I turned to look at him, too. He had a rigid smile that looked more like gas pains.

"Well?" I repeated.

"I—I don't—I'm not sure."

I turned to Eli Contini. "I guess that means it's time for Exhibit J."

Eli walked over to the wall and brought back the final wrapped poster.

As he set it on the easel, I said to him, "Just a moment, Mr. Contini."

Rubbing my chin thoughtfully, I turned toward the dress hanging from the hook. Then I looked over at the shoes and the purse resting on the ledge in front of Cissy Robb. Her eyes were wide as her gaze kept shifting from me to the wrapped poster on the easel to her lawyer and back to me again.

"Let me move these to a better position," I said.

I walked over to the dress and removed it from the hook. I carried it back to the easel and handed it to my client. "Mr. Contini, could you stand with the dress on this side of the easel?"

"Certainly."

I walked over to Cissy, who drew back as I approached, eyes wide. I picked up the fancy shoes and the handbag and carried them over to counsel's table, where I lined them up on the edge of the table near where Eli was standing. Then I stepped back, like a set designer, to study the arrangement. As I did, I glanced at the clock on the back wall.

12:11. Perfect.

I turned back to the judge with an apologetic smile. "Your Honor, I wonder if we could take a break? Before I move to the next line of inquiry, I would like to ask Mrs. Robb to put on the dress and the shoes."

Cissy gasped.

She was not alone. Stifled laughing could be clearly heard.

Howard Brenner was up like a jack-in-the-box. "Actually, Your Honor, if we're taking a break perhaps we could make it for lunch as well."

Judge Williams looked up at the clock and then back down at me with a knowing smile. "Very well, Mr. Brenner. Court will be in recess until two o'clock. That should give the plaintiff ample time to eat her lunch and put on the dress and shoes before she returns to the witness stand."

With a bang of her gavel, Judge Williams stood and left the bench as the bailiff called, "All rise!"

I glanced back at the gallery, where the gossip columnist and the society columnist were both typing on their cell phones. One row over I recognized a reporter from Channel 5. She smiled at me and rolled her eyes before turning toward the door to the hallway, her cell phone pressed against her ear.

As soon as the chambers door closed behind the judge, Eli Contini came over and hugged me.

"Oh, Rachel, *mazel tov*. You were magnificent."

"Not yet," I whispered. "It's not over."

"Still, Rachel—"

I shook my head and held up my hand in a stop signal. I nodded toward the other counsel table, where a grim Brenner and his associate were gathering their papers.

Cissy had left the witness box and was striding toward Brenner, clearly upset. Richie Robb intercepted her before she reached counsel's table. He grabbed her by the arm and marched her over to the empty jury box. He turned to glare at me and then leaned in close to Cissy, waving his arms angrily as he whispered to her.

I glanced at the easel, then back at Richie, who was now pointing at the easel.

"Wait," I said to Eli.

I walked over to the easel, took the wrapped poster board

marked DEFENDANT'S EXHIBIT J, and carried it over to the bailiff.

"Mr. Jamieson," I said in a low voice, "I need this locked up over the lunch recess,"

The bailiff was an elderly black man with a big paunch and a pleasant moon face. "Oh, that's okay, Miss Gold, we lock the courtroom doors during the lunch recess."

I leaned in close. "I can't leave it in here, Mr. Jamieson. I have to put it somewhere else."

He shrugged good-naturedly. "We can put it in the vault, Miss Gold. Follow me."

I told Eli to wait for me in the courtroom with his wife and son. "I'll be back in a few minutes. The bailiff won't lock up until then."

The vault was three floors down, inside the office of the Circuit Clerk. Once I got Exhibit J safely stowed, I walked down the hallway to a quiet area and called Jacki on my cell phone.

She'd been working on the subpoena to be served on the two wireless service providers—the one for the burner phone and the one for Isaiah's company phone.

"Hey," I said when she answered the phone.

"At last! I'm going crazy here. Tell me what's happening."

I filled her in on the morning's events.

"Oh, my God, Rachel, what if it doesn't work?"

"I'll improvise."

"Improvise?" She sounded apoplectic.

"I don't know. I'll have her stand there in the outfit—make sure my witnesses get a good look at her. Maybe it'll jog their memories about what she wore that night. And I always have Eli. He's a compelling witness. Don't worry, Jacki. I'll think of something."

"Don't worry? Are you kidding? I'm going into cardiac arrest over here. I'm coming down to court, Rachel. I have to be there."

Chapter Thirty-Six

I checked my watch when I got off the elevator. It was almost ten to one. According to the judge, we were in recess until two.

Although I didn't have an appetite, I could hear my mother's voice telling me I had to keep up my strength for the afternoon. Also, she would no doubt add, you have guests, doll baby—your client, your client's wife, and their son.

Yes, Mother.

I headed back to the courtroom to gather the Contini clan for a lunch somewhere near the courthouse. As I pushed through the door, Eli jumped to his feet. "Ah, Rachel, hurry. They're waiting for you in the judge's chambers."

I frowned. "Who's waiting?"

"Her lawyer and the judge. The clerk told me to send you back there immediately."

———

Thirty minutes later I emerged from Judge Williams' chambers and found Eli Contini pacing in the hallway while his wife and son watched from a bench. Jacki stood next to the bench, talking on her cell phone.

Eli came dashing over. "Well?"

I smiled. "I have a new settlement proposal from them."

He straightened. "What now?"

"Fifty thousand dollars."

He snorted. "I wouldn't pay that woman a dime."

"And you won't. Their opening offer was to drop the lawsuit in exchange for your agreement to keep the settlement terms confidential. I told them you were willing to keep the terms confidential but that you expected to be reimbursed for your time and your legal fees. They offered a thousand. I demanded one hundred. The judge convinced them to split the difference. I told them to wait while I sought your approval."

"What?" He gaped at me in astonishment. "*She* will pay *me* fifty thousand dollars?"

I nodded.

"And drop the lawsuit?"

I nodded again.

"Oh, my God," he mumbled. Then he stiffened, uncertain. "What are these confidential settlement terms?"

"One, we have to destroy all photographs of her, and, two, we can't let anyone know she paid you to get rid of the lawsuit."

There were tears in his eyes. "Rachel, I told you in your office that God smiles down upon you." He placed his hands on my shoulders and kissed me gently on each cheek. "Thank you, my dear."

We drew up the settlement papers right there in the courtroom. After both parties signed the settlement, the Contini clan, Jacki, and I left for a victory lunch at Eli's favorite Italian restaurant on the Hill.

During lunch I explained why the lawsuit would cost the Robbs far more than fifty-thousand dollars.

"The settlement terms may be confidential," I said, "but those reporters can put two and two together. Whatever social shame Cissy thought she'd crush with her lawsuit is only going to get worse. And that is bad news for Richie, too. Really bad news. I'm convinced he's the one who told her to return that dress. That's the only explanation for why he tried to bully me in the park. Assuming I'm right, I'm guessing Richie is not going to be sleeping in the master bedroom tonight."

Jacki laughed. "Or for the foreseeable future. What goes around comes around."

———

Brenner had promised to arrange for delivery to the restaurant of a fully executed copy of the settlement agreement along with a certified check for fifty thousand dollars. Both arrived during dessert. By then we were on our third bottle of Chianti.

"Ah," Eli said with a wistful smile, "I have only regret." He gazed at me across the table. "I wished I could have seen that woman's expression when you unveiled Exhibit J."

I glanced over at Jacki, who stifled a giggle.

I turned to Eli. "Then you have no regrets, Eli. No one would have ever seen that exhibit."

Eli frowned. "But it was the next one. It was on the easel. I put it there myself, my dear."

"You certainly did. But if trial had resumed after lunch, the easel would have been empty."

Now he was baffled. "I don't understand."

"Can you keep a secret?" I asked.

"Certainly."

I looked around the table and leaned forward. "Both of the photographers—the one for the *Post-Dispatch* and the one for the *Ladue News*—checked their photo files from that event. Neither one had a single picture of her that night. Not a one."

"But Exhibit J. What was it?"

I smiled. "A blank poster board."

Eli Contini looked at his wife and then back at me. "I don't understand."

Jacki leaned forward. "Have you ever played poker, Mr. Contini?"

He stared at her a moment and then leaned back in his chair and smiled at both of us. He raised his glass of wine. "To Rachel Gold and her magical Exhibit J."

I pressed my index finger to my lips. "Shhhh."

THE CIRCUIT COURT OF
ST. LOUIS COUNTY
(21st Judicial Circuit)
STATE OF MISSOURI

Friday Docket

Division R:
Judge Margaret Susan Gallagher
Final Pre-Trial Conference—1:30 p.m.
State of Missouri v. Holly B. Goodman,
Case No. 18SL-CR199436–02

Chapter Thirty-Seven

To waive or not to waive, that is the question.

I'd been searching for the correct answer ever since I got back to the office after my celebration lunch with the Continis—searching for that answer with Jacki, with Holly Goodman and her sister, Megan, with Benny, with my mother, and, of course, with myself.

But now, Friday afternoon, at the final pretrial conference before Circuit Judge Margaret Gallagher, my search had timed out. I had to answer.

"Your Honor," I said, "the defendant waives her right to a jury trial."

Judge Gallagher pursed her lips and glanced over at Sterling Walpole, who stood next to me at the podium. "Counsel?"

Walpole grinned and held his hands out, palms up. "The State is fine with that decision, Judge. We come before this honorable court seeking justice and, frankly, the sooner the better."

Judge Gallagher gazed at him for a moment, her expression stern, and then turned to the clerk. "Let the record show that the defendant waives a jury trial. We shall start this trial at ten a.m. on Monday."

There were not many judges in St. Louis County for whom I

would consider waiving a jury trial, but Margaret Gallagher was one of them. Now in her late fifties, she'd started her career as a public defender, switched sides a decade later to become a prosecutor, and was appointed a circuit judge ten years ago. During her years on the bench she had earned a reputation as a diligent and fair-minded judge—and one who did not appreciate clowning. Hers was a courtroom where the business of justice was serious business, as demonstrated by her deadpan reaction to Sterling Walpole's flippant attempt at humor.

That she had worked in the same office as Walpole for nearly a decade was a factor in my decision to waive a jury. And that she bore a striking resemblance to Miss Kelly, my favorite high school teacher, was probably another (perhaps embarrassing) factor. Like Miss Kelly, Margaret Gallagher was on the skinny side of slender, with angular features, thin lips, straight graying brown hair cut shoulder-length with bangs, and wire-rimmed glasses. And like Miss Kelly, Judge Gallagher projected an aura of conscientiousness.

"I have reviewed both of your witness lists," she said. "Ms. Gold, I see you have on your May Call List representatives from two mobile phone networks. Why is that?"

"One is the wireless service provider for the cell phone of the late Mr. Blumenthal, also known as Isaiah. The other is the wireless carrier for the mystery phone—namely, the one that sent the text messages to Mr. Blumenthal's cell phone. We don't have either report yet, but our hope is that they will be able to help the court pinpoint the location of that mystery phone at the time that each of the three texts was sent."

She turned to Walpole. "Counsel?"

Walpole chuckled. "I admire Miss Gold's diligence and determination, but I would point out to both her and this court that we assume that her client was not foolish enough to send those incriminating texts from her own house. And, thus if it turns out she sent them from some other location, we can all agree those facts would hardly exonerate her."

She turned to me. "Counsel?"

I smiled. "Mr. Walpole may be right about what we can all agree on, but he may be wrong. I'd prefer to see those reports before making any decisions."

The judge nodded. "I understand. When do you expect to have those reports?"

"I'm hoping by Monday, Your Honor. No later than Tuesday morning."

"Speaking of witnesses," Walpole said, "I note that Miss Gold has also included on her May Call List someone from the Security Desk operations at the MP Enterprises building in Clayton. Made me curious, Judge." He turned to me. "What's up with that?"

I kept my eyes focused on the judge. "Mr. Walpole is correct. I listed that representative on my May Call List. Per the Court's pretrial order, that is a list of witnesses that I may or may not call, depending upon the evidence the State puts on. I believe the attorney work-product privilege protects from disclosure the strategic reasoning behind my decision to include that potential witness on the list. Accordingly, Your Honor, I would respectfully request permission to decline answering Mr. Walpole's question."

"Permission granted."

"Thank you, Your Honor."

"Mr. Walpole," the judge said, "how long do you expect it will take for the State to put on its case in chief?"

"Now that we know we don't have to spend time picking a jury, I'm hoping to rest by lunchtime on Tuesday."

The judge nodded as she slowly flipped through the other pretrial filings. "Very good, Counsel. The Court will see you both at ten a.m. on Monday."

Chapter Thirty-Eight

"And, thus, Your Honor, the evidence will show beyond a reasonable doubt that the defendant had both the motive and the premeditated means to kill her brother."

Sterling Walpole paused to look over at me, shook his head sternly, and turned back to the judge. "Now I assume that counsel for the defendant will devote a good portion of her defense to demonstrating that the late Mr. Blumenthal was not exactly a warm and cuddly person. And the State is certainly not here to refute that evidence. Just because the late Mr. Blumenthal may not have been a saint does not justify his murder in cold blood. The criminal law of homicide makes no distinction between sinners and saints. And whether Mr. Blumenthal was the former or the latter or, like most of us, somewhere in between, killing him is still a crime."

Walpole paused, smiled, and nodded his head toward the judge. "That is all, Your Honor."

He stepped away from the podium and returned to counsel's table, giving me a pitying smile as he passed.

"Ms. Gold," Judge Gallagher said, "do you have an opening statement?"

I glanced at Holly Goodman, who was seated at our table

between Jacki and me, her head down. I stood. "Not now, Your Honor. Perhaps I'll have an opening statement after the State rests. But for now, we can proceed."

The judge nodded. "We will note that reservation of rights for the record."

She turned to Sterling, who was seated at the prosecutor's table with a junior assistant prosecutor on each side. "You may proceed, Mr. Walpole."

Walpole put on the State's case in a fairly straightforward manner, which is what I expected. His first witness was the medical examiner who had performed the autopsy on Isaiah. He testified that the cause of death was cyanide poisoning. His report was marked as Exhibit 1. I didn't bother with cross-examination.

The second witness was Ronald Carsen, the police detective who had, pursuant to the search warrant, seized the two containers of potassium cyanide—one sealed, one opened—from Holly's basement. Walpole took him through the chain of custody from the moment of seizure up to their presence in court and had them marked as exhibits.

"Nothing further, Judge."

She turned to me. "Counsel?"

I stood. "A few questions for the witness, Your Honor."

"Proceed."

I stepped to the podium. "Good morning, Detective."

He nodded. "Ma'am."

"You are aware that the medical examiner determined that Mr. Blumenthal died of cyanide poisoning, correct?"

"Yes, ma'am."

I turned to the two containers of potassium cyanide. "And these are the containers you found in the basement of Mrs. Goodman's home, correct?"

"Yes, ma'am."

"And the labels on those two containers state that they contain potassium cyanide, correct?"

"Yes, ma'am."

"And one of those containers—Trial Exhibit 6—was open at the time you found it in the basement, correct?"

"Yes, ma'am."

"Have you attempted to match the potassium cyanide in the open container with the cyanide found in Mr. Blumenthal's body?"

Detective Carson frowned. "Well, my understanding is—"

"I didn't ask for your understanding, Detective. I asked whether you attempted to match the contents of that open container with the form of cyanide found in Mr. Blumenthal's body. Yes or no?"

Carson shrugged. "No."

"Are you aware of anyone else on this case who has tried to match the contents of that open container with the form of cyanide found in Mr. Blumenthal's body?"

"Objection, Your Honor."

The judge turned to Walpole. "On what grounds?"

"Irrelevant. Come on. Cyanide is cyanide."

"Overruled." She turned to the witness, who leaned back, eyes widening. "Detective, counsel asked you whether you are aware of anyone else who has worked on this case matching the contents of that open container you found in the defendant's basement with the form of cyanide found in decedent's body. Yes or no?"

"No, ma'am. I'm not aware."

The judge turned back to me. "You may proceed, Ms. Gold."

"No further questions, Your Honor."

Chapter Thirty-Nine

The attorney conference rooms were located at the back of the courtroom, one on each side. We had the one on the left. Holly and I spent a few minutes alone in there at the beginning of the lunch recess. She was, understandably, distraught. I did my best to assure her that things were going okay so far.

We had ordered lunch from Potbelly's. When it arrived, Jacki knocked on the door and she and Megan joined us. Megan had been seated in the gallery during the morning proceedings. We passed out the sandwiches and drinks and settled in around the table.

"You had that detective squirming up there, Rachel," Megan said.

"I'm sure he's faced much tougher questioning than that," I said.

"Maybe, but he sure wasn't a happy puppy."

I looked at Jacki. "What about Walpole?"

"He seemed unfazed."

I turned to Holly. "That's good news."

"Really? Why?"

"It's what happens when the prosecution thinks they have a sure winner. They get overconfident. Just like the cops. They stop looking for more evidence—or scrutinizing what they have. Like with the cyanide. There's probably no way you could trace the cyanide in your brother's body to any particular container of that poison, but if that's so, they should have had either the medical examiner or that detective testify to that fact—or at least have them prepared for my question about it."

I turned to Jacki. "Like that burner phone. Classic example. They still haven't tried to get any location information for those texts."

"Why not?" Megan asked.

"Because Walpole is positive that Holly sent the texts. And as he said in court last Friday, they assume she was smart enough to send them from somewhere away from her house."

"Keep our fingers crossed on that one," Jacki said.

"When will you hear back?" I asked her.

"Later today. I've got meetings with each of them this afternoon."

"By the way," Megan said, "guess who I saw out in the court-house hall when we broke for lunch?"

"Who?" I asked.

"That Glasscock guy. The one who looked at the family albums."

"He's on their witness list," I said. "Actually, on ours, too. Just in case."

"Why do they want him?" Holly asked me.

"Those three texts. They can't make you testify, and they don't want to risk calling Megan. So I assume they're going to put Larry Glasscock on the stand. All three of those incidents are in his manuscript."

I turned to Jacki. "Another questionable strategy for them."

She smiled. "Agreed. You'll have some fun with him."

"Let's hope."

"What about Anna and the secretary and the Weasel and that fat tattooed redhead—the IT guy?" Megan asked. "Why are they here?"

"All four are on our witness list and on the prosecution's list.

Don't know whether Walpole plans to call any of them, but we served all four with subpoenas, so they had to show up today."

"Are you going to put them on the stand?" Megan asked.

"Haven't decided. We'll see how things play out."

"Those two women." Jacki shook her head. "Like poster girls for the RBF syndrome."

Holly frowned. "What's an RBF?"

"Initials," I said. "Resting Bitch Face."

Megan laughed. "Goddam right. Both of them for sure. Rachel, what's that Yiddish nickname you gave Haddock?"

"Frau Farbissina. But credit on that goes to Mike Myers."

We ate in silence as each of them checked their cell phones for messages, and I went over my trial notes.

There was a rap on the door.

"Come in," I called.

The judge's bailiff opened the door and peered inside. "Counsel, the judge will be ready to convene in five minutes."

We cleaned up the room and Megan and Jacki headed out of the room. I gave Holly a hug, gathered my notes, and started for the door.

Jacki was waiting just outside the conference room. She nodded toward the front of the courtroom. "Check it out."

Walpole's team had set up a display near the empty jury box. On a large easel facing the judge sat the following poster-sized chart:

THE THREE TEXT MESSAGES

Date	Time	The Text Message
June 24	**8:07 pm**	"Remember when I caught you wearing Mom's bra and panties? You've always been a total pervert and loser."
June 25	**4:40 pm**	"You were always evil and nasty. You even stole $20 from dad's wallet to buy firecrackers to light and throw at those poor dogs down the street. What a total creep you were—and you still are!"
June 27	**10:32 pm**	"You made your own parents ashamed that you were their son, like when you got drunk and threw up at Megan's *bat mitzvah* party. You've always been an embarrassment to our family."

"Well, well," Jacki said.

I nodded. "I like it better than our version. Should work for us."

"Let's hope."

Chapter Forty

Sterling Walpole spent a plodding ninety minutes walking Larry Glasscock through his manuscript of Isaiah's autobiography. Walpole asked him about the personal interviews, the drafting, the follow-up meetings with Isaiah to discuss edits and corrections to the manuscript. And then, one by one, he had Glasscock identify the passage of the manuscript that matched up with the information in each of the three text messages.

"And finally," Sterling said, "let's move to that third text. The one sent at 10:32 p.m. on June 27th—the day before the fateful mediation. As you will see, Mr. Glasscock, we have that text message in its entirety on the poster we have marked Exhibit Twelve. For the record, I will now read that text message: Quote—You made your own parents ashamed that you were their son, like when you got drunk and threw up at Megan's *bat mitzvah* party. You've always been an embarrassment to our family.—Close quote. Do you see that, Mr. Glasscock?"

"Yes."

"To the best of your knowledge, and based on your interviews with the decedent, does that text message describe a real event in the life of the deceased?"

"It does. Well, the first sentence does. I don't recall Isaiah telling me that he'd always been an embarrassment to his family. But he certainly viewed this moment, at the very least, as an embarrassment to himself."

"And did you include this event in the manuscript based on those interviews with the deceased?"

"I did."

"Please turn to the manuscript, which we have marked as Exhibit Fourteen. Can you find your description of the event described in that third text?"

Glasscock's copy of the manuscript had three yellow Post-it Note tabs, one for each of the relevant text messages. He flipped to the third one. "Yes. It starts on page ninety-four and continues over to the next page."

"Please read it aloud, Mr. Glasscock."

"Okay. It starts at the last paragraph on page ninety-four."

He cleared his throat. "Quote—Yet another low point on my sordid journey through adolescence occurred during my sister Megan's *bat mitzvah* dinner party, which took place at our country club. Underage access to alcoholic beverages at those parties was easy back then. No one carded you. And thus by the time the servers arrived with the dessert course, I had consumed at least five rum-and-Cokes. I had just chugged down the last one when my father stood to give his after-dinner speech to the more than two hundred family members, friends, and other guests. We were at the head table, which was on a raised platform so that all the guests could see us. I don't have a clear recollection of what came next. I do remember feeling dizzy and then nauseous and then the room tilted side to side as my father's voice droned on in the background. The voice faded away, followed by echoing sounds of applause. Then there was music. And then it happened. Suddenly. Horrendously. I leaned forward and spewed vomit onto the table and the dance floor, apparently splattering some of that puke onto my sisters and alarming the couples dancing the Macarena. I say apparently because I promptly passed out, sliding off the chair and onto the floor. Losing consciousness was probably the only positive of that disaster, since otherwise I would have been crushingly humiliated."

Glasscock looked up. "Do you want me to continue?"

Walpole chuckled. "No, sir. I think we've got the gist of that episode. Thank you. I have nothing further."

Judge Gallagher turned to me as I stood.

"I have some questions for the witness, Your Honor."

"Proceed."

I stepped to the podium. "Mr. Glasscock, MP Enterprises has produced in this case numerous emails between you and representatives of MP Enterprises regarding the autobiography project. None of those emails are between you and the deceased. Did you ever communicate with the deceased by email?"

"No."

"By telephone?"

"No."

"How were your interviews with him scheduled?"

"His secretary would schedule them by email."

I turned and pointed toward Mildred Haddock, who frowned at me. "By secretary, do you mean Ms. Haddock?"

"Yes. Her."

"How did you deliver the manuscript?"

"By email. I sent it to Ms. Haddock."

"Did you sign any agreements with Isaiah?"

"Yes. Two agreements. The one for the book and then a non-disclosure agreement."

"Who sent you those agreements?"

"His personal assistant. I think that's his title."

I turned and pointed toward Arnold Bell, who straightened in his seat. "Do you mean Mr. Bell, who is seated next to Ms. Haddock?"

"Yes, that gentlemen. He was the one who arranged the payments."

"And those payments were made at particular stages of the writing of the manuscript, correct?"

"Yes."

"So presumably someone at the company had to confirm that the manuscript had reached the next payment stage, correct?"

"I assume. I would send the notice—to Mr. Bell, I think—and the company would send me a check."

"The company has also produced emails in which the decedent's significant other, Anna, instructs Mr. Bell to personally fact-check the manuscript. Were you ever advised of that process?"

"Oh, yes. I believe it was Ms. Haddock who sent me correction pages that were the result of fact-checking by Mr. Bell and Miss, uh, Miss Anna."

"Let me show you what we have marked as Defense Exhibit E. Is that the email you received from Ms. Haddock with the correction pages?"

"Yes."

"Please read aloud the first two sentences of that email."

"Okay. Quote—The manuscript has been reviewed for accuracy by Mr. Bell and Anna. Attached are scanned copies of the correction pages—Close quote."

"Just to be clear, Mr. Glasscock, the prosecutor had you identify the passages in the manuscript that contained the information reflected in those three text messages on that poster, correct?"

"Yes."

"And thus anyone who read your manuscript would also learn the same information that is reflected in those three text messages on that poster, correct?"

"Objection, Your Honor! That calls for speculation."

The judge looked over at the poster with the three text messages as she rubbed the skin on her neck.

Then she turned back to Walpole. "Haven't you already established that very fact, Mr. Walpole?"

"I've merely established the truth of those three highly private text messages."

"And you established that truth by having Mr. Glasscock read the passages of the manuscript where the underlying facts behind each of those texts are set forth, correct?"

"Certainly, Your Honor, but that doesn't justify asking Mr. Glasscock to speculate about what someone else might learn from the manuscript."

As Judge Gallagher gazed at Sterling Walpole, I almost detected a hint of amusement in her eyes. "I agree, Mr. Walpole. We shouldn't speculate."

"Thank you, Your Honor."

"But I do have one question for you, Mr. Walpole."

Walpole grinned. "Fire away."

"How were you able to identify the three passages you had Mr. Glasscock read from his manuscript?"

Walpole frowned. "Pardon?"

"You had Mr. Glasscock read into the record three passages from his manuscript to establish the truth of the three text messages. My question, sir, is how did you identify those passages?"

"Well, I didn't do that personally. I had one of my able assistants review the manuscript and identify them for us." He looked at the assistant seated to the left at counsel's table. "Mr. Hormel, I believe."

That young man—presumably Mr. Hormel—nodded.

The judge said, "But then you read them yourself, correct."

Walpole smiled and nodded. "I most certainly did."

"And thus both you and your assistant, solely by reading those passages of the manuscript, learned the same information that is reflected in those three text messages on that poster, correct?"

Walpole looked perplexed.

"Correct, Mr. Walpole?"

"I suppose so."

The judge turned to me. "Do you still need the witness to answer that question, Counsel?"

I did my best to keep a straight face. "No, Your Honor."

I looked down at my notes. I had one more topic for Glasscock, but it was outside the scope of Walpole's direct examination and, more important, would have more resonance if I could cover it during presentation of our defense.

"No further questions, Your Honor."

"Mr. Walpole?"

Walpole leaned over to whisper with the assistant named Hormel. Then he nodded and turned to the bench as he stood. "Nothing further, Judge."

Chapter Forty-One

The morning of the second day of trial.

Sterling Walpole was waiting outside the courtroom as Jacki, Holly, and I approached.

He gave me one of his officious nods. "A word, Counsel?"

I looked at Jacki. "I'll meet you both inside."

She gave Walpole one of her stares—or more accurately, one of her glares. It had intimidated men far more macho than Walpole.

He forced a smile. "Miss Brand."

Without a word, Jacki opened the courtroom door and escorted Holly inside.

I turned to Walpole. "Okay. What?"

"The clock is ticking, Rachel."

"That's what clocks do, Sterling."

"But here that ticking clock means time is running out."

"On what?"

"On a deal. One helluva deal, if I say so myself."

"Which you just did. Cut to the chase, Sterling."

"Before the trial began, we were willing to recommend a plea for second-degree murder."

"And now?"

"I expect to rest the State's case today by noon. From now

until then, we are willing to recommend a plea for voluntary manslaughter. That is, to put it mildly, a truly generous offer in the context of the premeditated homicide your client committed. But when I announce that the State rests its case, that deal is off the table and we're back to first-degree murder. Think it over, Counselor. Carefully."

He gave me what I assume he believed to be an intimidating smile. "The clock is ticking."

———

And it kept ticking.

Walpole's final witness that morning was Mildred Haddock. She took the stand around eleven thirty. Her direct examination lasted just ten minutes. Her principal role as witness was to establish that Holly Goodman was alone in the conference room for approximately ten minutes while the Chairman wrapped up some business matter on the telephone.

She scowled at me from the witness box as I stepped to the podium.

"Good morning, Miss Haddock. As you know, my name is Rachel Gold. I have a few questions for you."

She leaned back in the chair and squinted.

"We first met back in May of this year," I said. "That's when you had requested me to meet with your boss. Do you recall that?"

"Yes."

"I met with him in his office, correct?"

"Yes."

"Early in that meeting he summoned you for a cup of coffee, and you brought him one in a stainless-steel mug with a black lid. Do you recall that?"

She frowned in thought. "Not clearly."

"Prior to that day, Miss Haddock, had the Chairman ever requested a cup of coffee?"

"Yes."

"More than once?"

"Yes."

"At least once or twice a week?"

"Yes."

"When he requested a cup of coffee, Miss Haddock, who would bring it to him?"

"Usually, I would."

"Usually? Who else would?"

She frowned as she thought it over. "Sometimes Mr. Bell. Sometimes, perhaps Anna. Sometimes, perhaps, someone else, especially if I was at lunch."

"Where would you get that coffee?"

She gave me a disdainful smile. "From the coffee maker."

"Where is that located?"

"In the small kitchen down the hall. Next to the conference room."

"Which conference room?"

She took a deep breath and shook her head. "The conference room where he was murdered."

"Who brewed the coffee in that small kitchen?"

"It depends."

"On what?"

"We have a kitchen staff downstairs. They check on the coffee makers on our floor periodically. Sometimes there is coffee when I go in there to pour some. Sometimes it's empty. When it is empty, I brew a fresh pot."

"As for that stainless-steel mug with a black lid that you brought your boss that day I was there, I assume that was not the only such mug, correct?"

She frowned. "What do you mean?"

"Is there more than one such mug?"

"Yes."

"How many?"

She pursed her lips. "At least five or six, maybe more."

"Are those mugs available for anyone to use?"

"No. They are strictly for the Chairman. They are stored on a special shelf in that small kitchen."

I nodded. "Let's go back to the day in question, Miss Haddock. According to Mrs. Goodman's sister, Megan Garber, the Chairman's coffee was there when she arrived. It was in a stainless-steel mug. He didn't show up for at least ten minutes. My question, ma'am, is who put that coffee mug in the conference room?"

Haddock frowned. "I'm not sure."

"Was it you?"

"I don't recall."

"Who else could it have been?"

She shook her head. "I don't know. Perhaps someone from the kitchen staff. I don't know."

"The same question when Mrs. Goodman was shown into the conference room. In fact, you were the one who met her at the conference room door, correct?"

"I believe so."

"And when she entered, that coffee mug was already there. With the lid on top. Did you put that coffee mug there?"

Haddock tilted her head to the side and rubbed her brow.

"Miss Haddock, did you put that coffee mug there?"

"I don't believe so. I can't recall for sure."

"Did you fill that coffee mug before Mrs. Goodman entered that conference room?"

A pause as she tried to recall. "I don't believe so. I don't believe so."

"Thank you, Miss Haddock. I have nothing further."

Chapter Forty-Two

We'd already established, through Glasscock's manuscript, that Isaiah's inner circle and Alonzo Flynn in IT had access to the highly personal information reflected in the three text messages. Thus, our first task after the State rested its case was to establish that Isaiah's inner circle, and possibly Flynn, also had access to the presence of cyanide in Holly's basement. That was a two-step process that began with J.R. Bates of Bates Inspections. Because I'd met with J.R. earlier, I handled his direct examination.

He was dressed the same as when we met at his office: tan work boots, faded jeans, and a blue chambray shirt. With his neatly trimmed goatee, dark hair combed straight back, and wire-rimmed glasses, all that was missing was the right headwear. Add a ten-gallon hat and he'd be Central Casting's answer for a cowboy. Swap out the hat for a beret and he'd be Central Casting's answer for a hipster poet.

I smiled as I watched the clerk administer the oath.

"...the whole truth, and nothing but the truth, so help you God?"

"I surely do, ma'am."

I walked him through the preliminaries—his background, his business, his home inspection methods, and his report format.

"Did you conduct an inspection of the home of Mrs. Holly Goodman?"

"Yes, ma'am."

"Do you recall the date of that inspection?"

"Honestly, I do not recall that date."

"I understand. Let me show you what we have marked as Defense Exhibit R."

I handed it to him.

"Do you recognize that document?"

"Yes, ma'am, I most surely do."

"Tell the Court what Defense Exhibit R is."

He turned to Judge Gallagher and held up the report. "This here, Your Honorable Mrs. Judge, is my inspection report on that house of Mrs. Holly Goodman, that nice lady over there seated at the table. The date of the inspection and the address of that house is right up here on the cover page."

After the judge admitted the exhibit into evidence, I asked, "For whom did you do that inspection and prepare that report?"

"Says right on the first page, Miss Gold. I did it for MP Financial."

"Did they tell you why that wanted you to do that work?"

"Yes, ma'am. It had to do with a refinance of that nice lady's home."

"Who was your contact at MP Financial?"

"That was a young lady by the name of Trotter. Real nice gal. Can't seem to recall her first name."

"That's okay. Mr. Bates, please turn to page eleven of your report."

"Okay, I'm there."

"Do you see that photograph?"

"Yes, ma'am, I do."

I turned toward counsel's table and nodded at Jacki, who was already on her feet and carrying a poster-sized document to the front. She placed it on a second easel, next to the one with the chart of the three text messages.

"Do you see that photograph that Ms. Brand just placed on the easel?"

"I do, ma'am."

"We've marked it Defense Exhibit S. Can you tell the Court what that exhibit is?"

"That appears to be a blowup of the photo right here on page eleven of my report."

"Why did you include that photo in your report?"

"As you can see, ma'am, there was a water stain on the wall just above that shelf with them containers on it. If you look at the text below that photo back in this here report, you'll see that I concluded that the stain appeared to be from an old water leak from a pipe that must have been repaired. I saw no evidence of recent leaking. I felt that was an important observation to include as part of my inspection report."

I turned to gaze at the blowup, glancing over to make sure that the judge was staring as well. The two containers of potassium cyanide were clearly visible on that top shelf.

I turned back to the witness. "Thank you, Mr. Bates. Nothing further."

"Mr. Walpole?"

Sterling was checking his notes. After a moment, he looked up and shook his head. "No cross, Your Honor." He smiled. "None needed."

The judge stared at him for what seemed a long time before she turned to the witness. "Thank you, Mr. Bates. You're excused."

As I sat down at counsel's table, Jacki stood and announced, "The defense calls Ms. Janice Trotter."

The bailiff walked to the courtroom door, opened it, and invited Janice Trotter in.

Jacki handled the direct examination and did a good job establishing the key points, namely, that Janice had been the loan officer on Holly's refinance application; that she'd ordered the inspection from J.R. Bates, with whom she had worked before and with whom she still works in her new position at US Bank; that she'd received and reviewed the inspection report from Bates Inspections; and that she had determined that the application, including the inspection report, met the requirements for a refinancing of the home loan.

"Did you approve the application?" Jacki asked her.

"I did."

"What happened next?"

"We understood that Mrs. Goodman was the sister of Mr. Blumen—uh, the Chairman of the parent company."

"Okay."

"So we thought it prudent to notify him of the loan application and our conclusions."

"How did you do that?"

"I sent my approval memo and the entire package upstairs to the executive suite."

"You said the entire package. Did that include the inspection report?"

"Yes, most definitely."

"To whom did you send it?"

"The Chairman's secretary. A Miss Haddock, I think."

"What happened next?"

She frowned and shook her head. "A few days later they sent back down my approval memo with the words 'application rejected' in thick black ink, like someone had written with a Magic Marker."

"Did anyone explain why the application was rejected?"

"No. I tried to find out but couldn't get an answer."

"You said that the approval memo was sent back down. What about the rest of the application package? Was that returned to you?"

"No."

"So they kept the inspection report?"

"I suppose. They certainly never sent that report back down."

I ended our day in court by putting Larry Glasscock back on the stand.

I did that in part so that he wouldn't have to come back to court again tomorrow but mostly because Jacki had received some promising news from the two wireless service providers during the break, along with confirmation from our expert witness that she would be available for tomorrow and could meet with us tonight. All of that meant that we could safely postpone the security guard testimony until the morning.

"Mr. Glasscock," I said, "I've handed you what the State marked yesterday as Exhibit Fourteen. As you see, that is a copy of the manuscript you wrote for Isaiah's autobiography, correct?"

"Yes."

"Please turn to the last page of the document."

I waited until Judge Gallagher had turned to that page on her copy of the manuscript.

"Do you see that reference to the purgatory of commerce?"

"I do."

"Were those his words or yours?"

Glasscock frowned and then looked up with a sheepish smile. "I guess you might say it was a combination."

"How so?"

"He'd decided to leave his company, including what he described as the vulgar world of commerce. He wanted to move on to something he felt was holier than commerce, more meaningful."

"Okay."

"We talked about those feelings. I happen to be a huge fan of Dante's *The Divine Comedy*. Don't know if you've ever read it. Anyway, it's a powerful work of poetry. I first read it back in college, and I've gone back to it several times over the years. As you may know, the narrator in *The Divine Comedy* starts his travels down in hell, which is known as the Inferno in the book. He then moves up to the region known as Purgatory—or, in Italian, *Purgatorio*. And the he finally reaches Paradise. Anyway, I told Isaiah about those three regions and he really liked the idea of dividing his life up into those phases. Purgatory would be his years at MP Enterprises."

"But he was going to leave the company?"

"Yes." He paused. "This was all confidential. His autobiography was not going to be published until he was actually gone from the company."

"Did he tell you when he was going to leave the company?"

"Not an exact date, but I got the sense it would be pretty soon. Maybe in a month or two. He'd already picked out where he was going to move. He'd already bought some land."

"Where."

"Initially, he was talking about moving west. Somewhere near Bend, Oregon."

"And what about the company?"

"He told me he was going to sell it to some foreign outfit."

I looked back down at the manuscript. "Now in the next paragraph on that last page, he states, and I quote, 'I have reached the next stage in my epic journey whence, guided by my own Beatrice, the lovely Anna, I shall leave purgatory behind and ascend to that paradise not of heaven but of this precious and fertile earth.'"

I looked up. "I assume Beatrice is a character from Dante's *The Divine Comedy*."

"Yes, she is the one in Heaven who sends Virgil out to lead Dante through the Inferno and Purgatory. Then she comes down to Purgatory to lead Dante up to Heaven or, as it's known in the book, *Paradiso*."

"So was Anna going to move out there with him?"

He smiled. "That's a good question."

"How so?"

"Well, I got the sense from him that Anna did not want to move. She didn't like the idea of trading her life in St. Louis for a new life out in rural Oregon. Sounded like they'd had some cross words about that. At some point, I think he changed the destination. He told me it was no longer Oregon. But he wouldn't tell me where. Still, he seemed pretty confident that he'd be able to change Anna's mind and make her go with him."

"What about his two assistants—Miss Haddock and Mr. Bell? Did he tell you what would happen to them after he moved?"

"Not really. I asked him once, but he just kind of shrugged it off and said they were adults and it was time they learned to take care of themselves."

"And finally, Mr. Glasscock, in all those private meetings you had with Isaiah, did he ever express to you any fear or concern that one of his sisters might try to kill him?"

"Objection. Irrelevant and hearsay."

"Overruled. I will allow him to answer. There is no jury here, Mr. Walpole. I can give his answer whatever worth I choose."

Glasscock frowned. "What was the question again?"

I asked the court reporter to read it back him.

"Fear or concern?" Glasscock chucked. "Isaiah? No, ma'am. Never."

Chapter Forty-Three

As Jacki, Holly, Megan, and I stepped off the courthouse elevator the next morning and walked past the usual gaggle of reporters and photographers shouting questions for us to ignore, I
was feeling surprisingly energetic—surprising because I'd had
maybe three hours of sleep the night before. It had been a crazy
evening, starting with dinner at my house. I'd missed my son,
Sammy, too much, having gotten home the prior four nights
long after my mother had put him to bed, only to leave in the
morning before he woke up.

I knew I had to be there for his bedtime last night, so I insisted
that Jacki and Benny, who'd volunteered to help with final trial
preparations, join us for dinner. Having given my mother advance
notice, she'd prepared a veritable Ashkenazi banquet: borscht
with sour cream, brisket, kasha varnishkes, carrot tzimmes, potato
knishes, and fruit compote. Jacki was a good sport, trying a little
of everything. Sammy was game for the brisket and potato knishes
but avoided the rest. Benny, however, was enraptured, scarfing
down massive quantities of each course as my mother watched
with approval. She beamed and nodded when he—after checking
with the rest of us—dumped the last four knishes onto his plate.

After dinner, Jacki and Benny went back to my office while I put Sammy to bed. I joined them around eight o'clock, which is when our expert witness arrived. We worked with her until almost ten thirty, Benny bowed out at eleven, and Jacki and I worked on trial prep until a little after midnight. I was in bed by one, tossed and turned until about two, woke up at five, and couldn't fall back asleep as I kept reviewing in my mind all the moving pieces for our presentation this morning.

Perhaps my energy was not surprising. I've learned over the years that being on trial is somewhat akin to what I've read about being a soldier on combat duty, without, of course, the added trauma of life-and-death perils. You don't get much sleep, you're under stress the whole time, but somehow the adrenaline keeps you going. And thus I felt pumped as we moved past the media mob and into the courtroom.

I put my arm around Holly as we walked toward our counsel table. She was holding up well, in part bolstered by her sister and in part by the way the balance seemed to be shifting during our phase of the trial. It was hard for me to assess Sterling Walpole's confidence in his case, though I took some comfort in his smug nod at me as we took our seats at counsel's table. It didn't appear, at least from his swagger, that he'd grasped the purpose of our witnesses yesterday, and especially the foundation they were helping us build for today, and thus I hoped he had no clue as to what was coming his way this morning. Seated in the first row behind the prosecutor's table were Anna, Arnold Bell, and Mildred Haddock. At the sight of me, the facial expressions of the two women morphed from RBF to outright contempt. Arnold just frowned.

At precisely nine a.m., Judge Gallagher entered the courtroom from her chambers and her bailiff ordered us all to rise.

When we were all seated again, the judge looked from me to Sterling and back to me, "Do we need to address any matters before the next witness?"

I stood. "None for the defense, Your Honor."

"Same for the State, Judge. We're good."

"Call your next witness, Ms. Gold."

"The defense calls Gordon Johnson."

A tall dignified black man in a gray suit, white shirt, and red-and-navy bow tie stepped toward the witness box. The clerk swore him in, he took his seat facing me, and we began.

"Good morning, Mr. Johnson."

"Good morning, ma'am." He had the sonorous voice of a preacher.

I walked him through the preliminaries—name, address, employment. Gordon Johnson was the head of security in the building housing MP Enterprises. I had him explain the rigorous clearance procedure for any visitor to the building.

"So just to be clear, Mr. Johnson," I said in summary, "if I came to the building to visit someone, you would first require me to give you my driver's license, which you would scan, and then you would call upstairs to the person I told you I was there to meet with, confirm that meeting, take my photograph, attach it to a visitor's pass that also had a unique bar code, and then, and only then, you would instruct me to pass through that security gate and enter one of the elevators, the operation of which you controlled from your security desk. In other words, if I was visiting someone on the ninth floor, and I passed all the security clearances, I would board the elevator you told me to board, the doors would close, and the elevator would rise on its own to the ninth floor. Have I accurately stated those procedures?"

"You have done so."

"Let me hand you the witness subpoena we've marked as Defense Exhibit R. As you know, that subpoena required you to bring certain documents to court today. Have you done so, Mr. Johnson?"

"I have."

"And did you give those documents to me when you arrived this morning?"

"I did."

"I've made copies for the judge and Mr. Walpole. Now the first category of documents requested in that subpoena was for any records regarding my entrance to the building on April nineteen. For the record, that was the day I met with the chairman of MP Enterprise. Did you find any such documents regarding that subject matter?"

"Yes, we did."

I approached the witness. "Let me show you what we've marked as Defense Exhibit U."

I handed copies to the judge and Walpole.

"What is Exhibit U, Mr. Johnson?"

"These are our records regarding your entrance to the building on that date. As you will see, they include a scanned copy of your Missouri driver's license, a copy of the photograph we took of you that day for your visitor's pass, and the confirmation from Miss Mildred Haddock that you did indeed have an appointment with the Chairman that morning. The time stamp is 9:54 a.m."

"Thank you, sir. There were four other dates in that subpoena, all concerning Holly Goodman. The first is for June twenty-eighth, which is the day of the mediation that ended with the Chairman's death. Did you locate any records regarding Ms. Goodman for that day?"

"I did."

I marked as an exhibit and had him identify the records for Holly's arrival that day—records similar to mine, showing her arrival at 8:36 a.m.

"As for the other three dates, Mr. Johnson, I direct you to the blowup chart on this easel. The State has marked the chart Exhibit Twelve. As you will see, there are three dates on that exhibit, each of which match with one of the other three dates in the subpoena."

Everyone turned to look at the chart:

THE THREE TEXT MESSAGES

Date	Time	The Text Message
June 24	**8:07 pm**	"Remember when I caught you wearing Mom's bra and panties? You've always been a total pervert and loser."
June 25	**4:40 pm**	"You were always evil and nasty. You even stole $20 from dad's wallet to buy firecrackers to light and throw at those poor dogs down the street. What a total creep you were—and you still are!"
June 27	**10:32 pm**	"You made your own parents ashamed that you were their son, like when you got drunk and threw up at Megan's *bat mitzvah* party. You've always been an embarrassment to our family."

"Mr. Johnson, according to your security records, did Ms. Goodman enter your building at any time on June 24th?"

"No, ma'am. We have nothing regarding Ms. Goodman for that day."

"Same question for June 25th?"

"Same answer. We have nothing regarding Ms. Goodman for that day."

"What about June 27th?"

"Again, no records regarding her, ma'am."

"Based on your security records, Mr. Johnson, can you confirm that Ms. Goodman did not enter your building on June 24th, 25th, and 27th?"

"Good Lord, Your Honor." Walpole was shaking his head in exasperation. "Enough is enough. Even though this is completely irrelevant and thus objectionable, in order to move this case along the State will stipulate for the record that the defendant was not in the building on any of those three days."

The judge turned to me. "Ms. Gold?"

"We will accept that stipulation, Your Honor. I have no further questions."

"Mr. Walpole."

Walpole, who was still standing, glanced down at his male assistant, who shook his head. He turned back to the judge.

"Nothing, Your Honor. Not a single question. And we restate our objection to this testimony as completely irrelevant to any issue in the case. We have never contended that the defendant entered the building on any of those three dates."

The judge turned to me. "Ms. Gold?"

"If the Court will bear with us, I promise we will connect Mr. Johnson's testimony directly to our defense."

She nodded. "Very well. I'll give you a little leeway on this, Counsel. But not much."

"Understood. Thank you, Your Honor."

Chapter Forty-Four

Next up were the witnesses from the two wireless service providers, each of whom had been subpoenaed for records concerning the location indicators for the burner cell phone at the precise time of the sending of each of the three text messages. Jacki handled their testimony as I took careful notes.

The first witness was a young woman from Freedom Mobile, the service provider for the burner phone. The second witness was an older man from MidwestCellular, the service provider for Isaiah's cell phone and the cell phones of the other MP Enterprises employees at the company's headquarters.

The Freedom Mobile witness gave a brief overview of how her company gathered geolocation data. As she explained, the relevant information occurs when a cell phone communicates with a cell tower, which occurs when that phone is used to call or text someone. She explained how the accuracy increases depending upon the number of cell towers that communicate with the phone on the particular call or text. When it communicates with just one cell tower, that information narrows the geographic range of the cell phone location to maybe a ten-mile radius. At the other extreme, where the phone communicates with three cell towers, the location range is narrowed to less than half a mile.

Fortunately, she explained, the likelihood of a three-cell-tower communication was fairly high in a region with a population density of metropolitan St. Louis, and thus the geolocation data Freedom Mobile obtained for all three text messages was the result of triangulation between three cell towers.

The same was true for the MidwestCellular information, as confirmed by that carrier's witness.

Both companies had downloaded the requested data, which came in the form of inscrutable sets of latitude and longitude numbers—or at least inscrutable to us non-cartographers. According to those records, all three messages were sent from a latitude that began with the number thirty-eight followed by a decimal point and six numbers and from a longitude that began with the number minus-ninety followed by a decimal and six numbers. Thus, for example, the Freedom Mobile provider for the burner cell placed the location of that burner cell at the time of the second text at the following geographic location:

Latitude: 38.650823

Longitude: -90.324925

The MidwestCellular provider for Isaiah's cell phone had similar but not identical numbers for the latitude and longitude of that same text message from the burner phone. Both witnesses cautioned that those latitude and longitude numbers were accurate to an area of plus-or-minus one quarter of a mile.

By the time the second witness left the stand, Jacki had scrawled on the whiteboard flip chart enough eight-digit latitude and longitude numbers to leave the judge and the rest of courtroom baffled. Baffled, but—I hoped—curious.

As Jacki prepared the laptop computer on the ledge of the witness stand and tested it with the widescreen monitor we'd arranged in front of the empty jury box facing the judge, I surveyed the crowded courtroom. My gaze paused at the first row behind the prosecutor's table, where Anna, Arnold Bell, and Mildred Haddock were still seated side by side. Anna met my gaze and shook her head. I noticed that Alonzo Flynn was now in the gallery as well, seated along the aisle near the back row. He was staring at the coordinate numbers Jacki had written on the whiteboard.

I turned toward our counsel table, where Holly sat alone as Jacki fiddled with the computer. Holly looked at me, the strain evident. I gave her a slight nod and a wink. She forced a smile. I looked over at Jacki, who had finished testing the computer at the witness box and was walking back to our table.

"All set," she said.

I turned to Judge Gallagher. "The defense calls to the witness stand Professor Evelyn Stengel."

Chapter Forty-Five

Rising from the back row of the gallery, a tall slender woman in a black single-button pantsuit started down the aisle. Professor Evelyn Stengel was in her forties and wore her dark hair pulled back in a short ponytail. Her strong attractive features were framed by an elegant pair of black horn-rimmed glasses. In her right hand she held a manila folder. She nodded at me as she strode past to the witness box, where the clerk swore her in.

"Good morning, Professor," I said.

"Good morning, Ms. Gold."

"Let's start with your full name, profession, your title."

"Certainly. My name is Evelyn Greene Stengel. I am a tenured professor in the Geography Department at the University of Missouri in St. Louis."

"Do you have an area of specialty within the field of geography?"

"I do. My academic focus is cartography, which is the science and art of the conception, production, dissemination, and study of maps."

I walked her through her expert witness credentials—academic degrees, job experience (including four years as a cartographer with the National Parks Service), her publications, and her honors.

I gestured toward the poster with the times and contents of the three text messages.

"Professor Stengel, let's turn to the question of the locations of this mystery burner cell phone at the time of each of these three texts. You were in the courtroom to hear the testimony of the witnesses from the two wireless service providers, correct?"

"Yes."

"And you have had an opportunity to review the materials produced by those two service providers in response to the subpoenas and that were marked earlier today as trial exhibits, correct?"

"Yes. Your colleague, Ms. Brand, provided copies of those materials to me yesterday."

"Have you done any further work in determining a more precise location for the cell phone at the time of the sending of each of those three text messages?"

"I have."

"Please describe that work, Professor."

"May I use that whiteboard?"

"Certainly."

Over the next ten minutes, Professor Stengel walked the judge and the rest of us through a beginning class in cell phone geolocation strategies, filling the whiteboard with a series of intersecting circles and dotted lines to explain her procedure for determining a more precise location for the three texts through her evaluation of the materials produced by the two wireless service providers.

"And that," she said, turning to face the judge, "is the analysis I performed."

I waited until she returned to the witness box.

"Professor, as a result of this analysis, have you formed an opinion as to the location of the burner cell phone at the time each of the three text messages was sent?"

"Yes, I have."

"In what format have you expressed that opinion?"

"As a cartographer, I created a map for each text message with the location of the cell phone highlighted with a red dot."

"And what does red dot represent?"

"Based on my research and evaluation of the materials produced by the two cell phone network carriers, I am confident the cell phone was located within a twenty-five-meter radius of the red dot on the map at the time that text message was sent."

"Did you bring those maps with you?"

"Yes."

"In what format?"

She gestured toward the laptop. "I created them on this computer and then I printed them out."

She lifted the manila folder. "Unfortunately, I didn't have access to a color printer, so these images are not as clear in black-and-white. But with this computer I can display the three maps in color on that large monitor over there, which will also enable me to zoom in and out of the maps."

"Can I have black-and-white copies to distribute?"

"Certainly." She handed the folder to the clerk, who handed it to me.

I sorted through the pages, handing three to Walpole, three to the clerk for the judge, and three to the witness.

I returned to the podium. "Professor, as you will see, I have given you back the three printed maps marked as Defense Exhibits W-1, W-2, and W-3."

"Yes, I see that."

"Let me direct your attention to this poster on the easel marked Exhibit Twelve."

All eyes turned toward that poster:

THE THREE TEXT MESSAGES

Date	Time	The Text Message
June 24	**8:07 pm**	"Remember when I caught you wearing Mom's bra and panties? You've always been a total pervert and loser."
June 25	**4:40 pm**	"You were always evil and nasty. You even stole $20 from dad's wallet to buy firecrackers to light and throw at those poor dogs down the street. What a total creep you were—and you still are!"
June 27	**10:32 pm**	"You made your own parents ashamed that you were their son, like when you got drunk and threw up at Megan's *bat mitzvah* party. You've always been an embarrassment to our family"

"Let's begin with that second text message—the one sent on June 25th. I believe the map you created for that is Exhibit W-2, correct."

She looked at the map and nodded. "Yes."

"Using your computer, please display the color version of that map on the monitor."

"Okay. I should point out that when the map opens, the view will be from fairly high up, but we will be able to zoom in closer."

She tapped a few keys on the computer and the widescreen monitor lit up with a high-definition color version of the map.

I said nothing, letting the judge and all the others in the court-room try to orient themselves to what was on the monitor screen. That map was indeed zoomed out—so far out that the exact position of that red dot was hard to pinpoint beyond its general location west of the Mississippi River and south of the Missouri River, although significantly closer to the former.

"Now I will move us in closer," she said, tapping on the key-board as she watched the screen.

As the view zoomed in, the red dot and surrounding area expanded rapidly until we were staring at a specific location on a specific street in downtown Clayton, Missouri.

There was a moment of silence, and then some whispered chatter in the gallery. I glanced over at the prosecution table, where Sterling Walpole was squinting at the screen and shaking his head. Then I looked at the judge, who was studying the image on the monitor.

"Professor, what is the address of where that red dot is located?"

She gave the address.

"What is located at that address?"

"That is the building housing the headquarters of MP Enterprises."

More hushed chatter from the gallery.

"To be clear, Professor Stengel, is it your expert opinion that the text message sent to Isaiah's cell phone at 4:40 in the afternoon on June 25th was sent from the headquarters of MP Enterprises?"

"Yes, that is my opinion. Obviously, I can't determine the floor from where it was sent, but the various geolocators confirm that it was sent from that location."

I paused to let the onlookers—and especially Judge Gallagher—absorb the significance of that fact.

"Okay, Professor, let's now move to the text sent the day before at seven minutes before eight p.m. This is the black-and-white exhibit we have marked as Exhibit W-1. Please display that map on the monitor."

And once again we started with a view of the red dot from far above the city. When she zoomed in, we were on a street named Hoyne Avenue in the suburban town of Kirkwood.

"It appears that the red dot is located about two-thirds of the way down that street," I said.

"Yes," she said. "Unlike the office building where MP Enterprises is located, the homes in that area are much smaller. Thus the closest I can locate that cell phone is along Hoyne within the fourth, fifth, or possibly the sixth house from the western end of that block."

"What are the addresses for those three houses on Hoyne?"

"Twenty-Seven Hoyne, Twenty-Nine Hoyne, and Thirty-One Hoyne."

We then moved to the last of the three text messages—the one sent on the night before the mediation. The location of the cell phone for that text was the same as the first text—namely, one of the three houses on Hoyne Avenue.

"Thank you, Professor. Nothing further."

"Mr. Walpole?" the judge asked.

Walpole huddled with his two assistants for a moment and then turned to the judge and shook his head, clearly rattled. "No questions."

"Thank you, Professor," Judge Gallagher said. "You are excused."

She turned to me. "Ms. Gold? Any more witnesses?"

"Just one more, Your Honor. The defense calls to the witness stand Arnold Bell."

There were some muffled gasps.

I waited, checking my notes, facing forward.

"Mr. Bell?" the judge finally called. "Is Mr. Arnold Bell here?"

I turned toward the gallery.

When Professor Stengel had taken the stand, Arnold Bell was seated between Mildred Haddock and Anna.

He was no longer there.

Chapter Forty-Six

As you probably surmised, one of those three addresses on Hoyne is—or rather, was—the residence of Arnold Bell, who lived alone in the two-bedroom ranch house at Twenty-Seven Hoyne Avenue. The following evening the police found his corpse facedown on his kitchen floor in a pool of vomit. A note in Bell's handwriting taped to the kitchen table read: "Revenge is a drink best served hot. He deserved to die, and so do I."

The medical examiner would later determine the cause of death as cyanide poisoning, and the police would confirm that the container of potassium cyanide on the kitchen counter had been purchased online by Arnold Bell three weeks earlier. In a file cabinet in his basement they would find the missing inspection report on Holly's home. The report's photograph of the two cyanide containers on the basement shelf beneath the water stain had been circled in red. Although Bell left no explanation beyond the two-sentence suicide note, my guess is that after years of abuse—even worse than what I had witnessed, such as a batch of vicious, disparaging emails from Isaiah that Bell had printed and saved in that same file cabinet—the final trigger for revenge had been his discovery of Isaiah's plan to sell the company and essentially abandon him. The killing of Isaiah also killed that sale, but it eventually killed the killer as well.

But back to the criminal case, which Judge Gallagher dismissed later that Thursday afternoon. The following night Holly and her two teenage daughters, Megan and her two teenage daughters, and Jacki and I gathered in a private dining room at Holly's favorite restaurant for a celebratory dinner. Holly and Megan, now co-trustees of their mother's trust, were delighted to pick up the tab, and I was delighted to finally go home for a weekend without another trial to prepare for.

Nevertheless, as any working lawyer will confirm, the end of a big trial or the closing of a big transaction just means that you will return to the office with voice mail messages and emails from clients with "urgent" matters needing your "immediate" attention. I listened to those voice mails, read those emails, and made a decision that none of them required a response before Monday.

I made one more decision as I drove home from that Friday night victory dinner, a decision I had been contemplating for some time.

The next morning I dropped Sam off at Central Reform for religious school. Abe Rosen had already parked in the lot and, as was our usual routine, was walking over to my car for the drive to Osage Café for our Saturday morning *kaffeeklatsch*. And, as usual, he looked handsome and sexy as he climbed in on the passenger side.

"Good Shabbos, Rachel."

"Good Shabbos to you, too, Abe. And thanks for those flowers. That was so sweet."

"You deserved them. Your victory made the front page of the *Post-Dispatch* and the lead story on the news that night. I'm so proud."

I pulled out of the carpool lane onto Waterman and stopped at the red light at Kingshighway. When the light changed to green, I turned right.

"Isn't Osage to the left?" Abe said.

"It is. I thought of a better spot for coffee."

"Okay. Where?"

"You'll see."

Ten minutes later, I pulled into my driveway and drove around to the back door. I put the car in park, killed the engine, and turned to Abe.

He gave me a puzzled smile. "We're having coffee here?"

"Coffee? Well, that all depends." I checked my watch. "We have ninety minutes before we need to pick up the kids."

I leaned over and gave him a soft kiss. "If we run out of time, the next cup is on me."

He smiled. "That's a deal."

And as I got out of the car I had to admit to myself that sometimes—not always, not usually, but sometimes—my mother is right. There is, as she quoted Ecclesiastes, a time to every purpose under heaven.

ACKNOWLEDGMENTS

A special thanks to Barbara Peters and Annette Rogers, my two kind and insightful editors.

ABOUT THE AUTHOR

Photo by Alexandra Schenck

Michael A. Kahn is a trial lawyer by day and an author at night. He wrote his first novel, *Grave Designs*, on a challenge from his wife, Margi, who got tired of listening to the same answer whenever she asked him about a book he was reading. "Not bad," he would say, "but I could write a better book than that." "Then write one," she finally said, "or please shut up." So he shut up—no easy task for an attorney—and then he wrote one.

Kahn is the award-winning author of ten Rachel Gold mysteries, three stand-alone novels *Played!*, *The Sirena Quest*, and *The Mourning Sexton* (under the pen name Michael Baron)—and several short stories.

In addition to his day job as a lawyer, he is an adjunct professor of law at Washington University in St. Louis, where he teaches a class on censorship and free expression. Married to his high school sweetheart, he is the father of five and the grandfather of, so far, seven.

See his website at: michaelakahn.com.